ANTISOCIETIES

Michael Cisco

GRIMSCRIBE
PRESS

New Orleans, Louisiana

Published by
Grimscribe Press
New Orleans, LA
USA

grimscribepress.com

CONTENTS

Intentionally Left Blank

W E LIVED IN a little house on the hilltop, just below the peak. Nobody lived up on the actual ridge line. There was a narrow, snaky side street that went up and around one curve, and we all were hidden up at the end of it, a cluster of maybe a dozen small houses. Everybody knew each other, because we formed a kind of pocket community up there. With no through traffic, people would be out in the street all the time. We were a sociable bunch up there. If I put my mind to it, I imagine I could probably remember the family name of each home.

That year, my mother tried to kill herself and had to go into the hospital for a while. My father had to go back to base at the same time and couldn't get an exemption, so Aunt Gabrielle offered to take me in for the time being. She lived in a white stucco house on the hilltop, nestled in a heavy spiderweb of cables. I remember there were cables strung up all over, so that it looked as though the houses were all leashed to each other. People were in and out of that house all the time, because she was in a wheelchair and never left the hill. This guy named Claudio she called her "boyfriend" did all the shopping; he was a musician who lived somewhere in the valley, but he came by pretty often and took good care of her. She had two refrigerators, a big lie-down deep freezer, and a garage full of food in cans and boxes, enough to feed an army, so I wasn't any burden. It meant stale cereal and microwaved stew, dusty two-liter bottles of soda and angel food cake you had to thaw out in the microwave at two in the morning with a pillow over the oven so the beeping wouldn't wake her up, that's all. She wouldn't have complained if I had woken her up.

I was between schools, but it was summer anyway. The main problem was that I had no way of getting around, and there was no one my age in the little cluster of houses. Most of the people there were either young or old, with almost nobody in the middle. I think the youngest adult there was maybe in their forties, and he was a flat-top, sort of strait-laced, frumpy math teacher guy who dedicated his life to his lawn. So, I was kind of stuck there, with not much to do, and that's how things turned out the way they turned out. I wanted to turn inward and get monastic with video games or guitar practice, something like that, but I suck at guitar and Aunt Gabrielle had exactly one "computer device" in the house and that was hers. There was a doily on top of it. I just had my phone.

Plus, the neighbors were always coming by. The house was small, although the guest room was sort of angled out from the rest of the house, protruding a bit over the edge of the hill, so I could sit in there without hearing absolutely every word they were saying. Sometimes a visitor would break away to go to the bathroom, and the conversation would swerve in my direction, then cut off abruptly. Toilet flush. Pause. Hopefully the sound of the tap running. Then the talk would resume and dwindle back toward the kitchen. From my room, I could see into the back yard of Dr. Wilson, who was a retired dentist, living next door. He had a garden and a sheltering structure for an old-time sports car roadster I never saw completely. Dr. Wilson came by every day to say hello to Aunt Gabrielle and recommend dentistry and the military to me.

"You'd be amazed at how tightly it tends to run in families," he'd say. He was a soft-spoken man in his sixties (I think) with iron-grey hair, a deep tan. Sort of a golfer type. He'd been in the navy. I would see him sometimes jogging up that steep hill. He kept himself in shape. Once he loaned me a book about the Civil War—he was hugely interested in the Civil War. I started avoiding him after that. I didn't want to tell that I hadn't read it and didn't care; I guess I was afraid of hurting his feelings.

This isn't local color or whatever; it matters. You have to understand that Dr. Wilson was totally ordinary. Just bear with me, and you'll get why that matters in a moment.

Like I said, I could see into his yard from my room. We were a little higher than his house, so I could see down into it. So, I would see him back there, doing chores from time to time. He went back to his garage a lot, and now we're getting into it. Every now and then I'd hear him talking, and once I glanced outside and he was coming out of the garage, talking, not on a phone, but to someone else who was still inside the garage. There was no doubt about it; he was clearly telling someone something that had only just occurred to him as he was leaving. He used to do that with my Aunt Gabrielle, so that you couldn't be sure when he was getting ready to go or getting ready to launch into another long bit about photography, the Civil War, football. He was doing that with someone in his garage, though, even though he lived alone. I mean, no one told me he lived alone, but no one ever mentioned anyone else living there with him. I think he was saying something about remembering to do this or that, like he was giving someone advice about a task. It's one of those memories you forget until something makes you remember, and you come back to it and see it in a new light.

What made me remember that was seeing him working on the car with someone else, maybe a week later. There were tarps up, hanging from a frame that suspended them over the car, so I couldn't see much of the other person, only that it was someone big, but once they came around to the nearer side and I saw their shadow through the tarp, and they had some kind of wiggly things sticking out of their head. I couldn't figure it out. It was weird. So, I remembered it. And I wondered if that was the person in the garage.

I actually saw who it was without realizing it. It was around the same time. I was out getting the mail, and I saw Dr. Wilson cross his kitchen window, and someone else was there too, just moving out of sight as I looked up. At the time, I didn't think about it. Dr. Wilson was as sociable as my Aunt Gabrielle, and neighbors visited him all the time, too, so I assumed it was some neighbor. But, looking back, I recognize the shapeless purple sweater that person was wearing; because, that day with the car, I saw part of the other person, an arm in a raggedy purple sweater sleeve, reaching around the front of the car while the person was crouching beside Dr. Wilson. Does that make sense? I mean, the person was wearing that same sweater, not just one that was the same color. It was beat up the same way, and even dirty, too, like something you'd see somebody homeless wearing. I wondered if maybe Dr. Wilson let somebody homeless stay with him or help him out with chores, like work-for-food? But then I remembered the weird springy head thing from the other day and didn't know what to think. Some big raggedy guy was living with Dr. Wilson, doing chores for him, and they had wiggly things sticking out of their head at least one time, and nobody ever mentioned him.

I got the good look at them that you're waiting to hear about a few days after that. I looked out my window and saw a big person in sort of rust-colored pants and boots and sagging purple sweater working in Dr. Wilson's garden. They had on floppy, colorless gardening gloves, and I guess they were weeding, in no hurry, kneeling on the ground, and they had on a rubber Halloween mask over their head. When they turned around to get the hand-rake thing, I saw the face and thought at first it was a green gorilla mask, or then a zombie, with the mouth hanging open, not in a snarl, but just open, like mindless.

Then I saw the snake heads wiggling in the shaggy fake hair, and it was a Medusa mask. The mouth was open, but there was backing inside it so you couldn't see the mouth inside. The eyes were filled in with staring Medusa eyes, sort of sloppily painted there with paint like two splashes of bird shit. There were slits under the eyes, so I guess you see out through those. And right away, I remembered the weird shapes around the silhouette of the head the other day. You see? It means they were wearing the mask then, when they were working on the car with Dr. Wilson. I didn't see the head that day through the kitchen window, but I sort of think that I saw the back of the mask, the scruffy, fake hair sticking out in all directions, just for a flash there. So, it's like they were in the same cheap, Halloween-store Medusa mask all the time.

Gee, what's under the mask, are they too gross under the mask and so they wear the mask, but why wear a cheap, shitty drugstore mask and not just like some kind of medical mask they make for people with facial deformities?

Dr. Wilson came out into the yard a moment later and started talking to them. You in the Medusa mask knelt on the ground listening and you nodded when Dr. Wilson was done. Then you went back to weeding. Aunt Gabrielle was talking with Mrs. Figiel from across the street when I came in and asked her what the deal was with the Medusa masked person next door, and she said she hadn't noticed anybody.

"Oh, you mean Dr. Wilson's friend?" Mrs. Figiel said.

"I don't know," I said. "I don't know who it is."

"Sort of big?" she said. "Works around the house, in the garden? And on that car he has, too, I think, right?"

"Do they always wear a mask? A Medusa mask?"

"You know, I think they do. I think they do usually have that mask on, yeah."

"Oh!" my Aunt said. "I know who you mean! They've been living with Mr. Wilson since before I moved here."

"And they always have that mask on?"

"I guess so," she said.

They couldn't tell me anything about them. They hadn't ever spoken with them, although, as my Aunt pointed out, they wouldn't likely know they had or hadn't, because they didn't know what their face looked like. But neither thought they had. If they changed out of their work clothes and went passing on the street, someone might well have waved hello, exchanged the usual pleasantries about the weather. My aunt's lack of concern didn't rub off on me; I pulled my shades down and stopped looking out the window of my room. I didn't want to see that rubber face with bird shit eyes again. When I heard Dr. Wilson talking next door, I turned up my headphones or stopped reading and stuck my head under my pillow, but it was like I could feel them out there, in that stifling mask with only the narrow eye slits, no opening in the mouth, breathing in the rank rubber smell, the headachy stink of the paint and the glue and stale breath. I caught another glimpse of them one night, coming around Dr. Wilson's house from the back yard, hauling out the trash can to the curb. A big guy, who carried themself with the impatient, heavy step I associated with maintenance men and construction workers. The livid green of the mask was flushed blue with the twilight. I turned my head away and went inside quickly, but I worried that they'd seen me do it and realized I hadn't wanted to look at them and might resent it. They'd never made any sound that I'd heard, not any vocal sound. I don't know why I did it. I acted without thinking. I turned back. They'd finished with the trash and were striding back toward the rear of Dr. Wilson's house.

"Hey," I called. I kept repeating it, but they didn't turn around. They just vanished around the corner.

Later that night, with my lights out, I spied out on Dr. Wilson's yard, hiding myself with the blind down. The lawn was black, the overhanging trees were black, the garage, like Dr. Wilson's house, was all rough, rustic-style dark planking with white trim. There was one window in the garage on this side, and it was dark, but suddenly I knew they were in there, wearing their Medusa mask. There was something darker in the window, with two pale spots on it. It could have been the mask, sitting on a shelf, or it could have been them, sitting perfectly still. There was no sound but the overlapped pulses of crickets at first. Then I heard a coyote yipping into the sky somewhere up on the ridge. He kept yipping out into the night. I waited to hear if any others joined in. None did. So, that was me, peering around the shade into Dr. Wilson's indigo yard, seeing Medusa mask sitting motionless at the window of the darkened garage, hearing that coyote's unanswered, shrill cries waver up in the neutral wash of cricket static.

I saw them nearly every day after that, always doing something around Dr. Wilson's place, in plain view. Everyone was used to Medusa mask but me. My Aunt Gabrielle recruited me to help her prepare what she called a "wing ding" so I tidied up and dusted her figurines and went to get supplies at the store with Mrs. Figiel and her son Dominic who only wanted to talk about metal. I saw the people stocking shelves at the store and stomping back to the inventory to get more, and people clearing brush along the side of the road in the blazing heat and orange vests and helmets, and guys in oily coveralls slapping their hands together and smoking out in front of the auto body shop, and I saw the Halloween store, somehow still open in the middle of summer. The "wing ding" happened, and all sorts of neighbors came to eat my Aunt's chicken wings from paper plates. Dr. Wilson showed up to say hi and apologize.

"My son threw his back out doing some yard work the other day, and I wanted to go check in on him. I'm sure it's nothing serious, but he's all alone out there while Lily's back east. She's a tax adjuster."

He looked at me.

"Fascinating job. I could tell you about it some time."

"Sure," I said.

He left. All the hobnobbing was getting me down, so I went back to my room. Shades down. I peeked around them. Medusa mask was bent over the car, with a toolbox open next to them. I began to wonder if I was strange for caring. Nobody else paid any mind. Why did this bother me so much?

Why doesn't it bother them? That's the question, I told myself. How is this normal? Again, I wanted to call out, and again something in me really wouldn't. I was starting to be frightened of what I might do, that I had this impulse to call out riding around in me.

I slipped out the back door and made my way to the street through the bit of scrub that divided my Aunt's property from the Overbrooks' next door. I walked up around the bend, maneuvered around the yellow gate that marked the end of the street and the beginning of the ridge trail, and spent a while up there by myself in the dust and brush. I wondered when they would notice I wasn't around.

The feeling started when I turned back. My heart felt like it was packed in hot mud. Hot mud that started to go cold right away and stayed cold. I was down like I had never been before, not further down. I mean, I'd been hurt much worse. I'd been more deeply sad than this, but this was just different. Like I knew something was coming, and I was going to be a part of it. I was going to be all about it, and it was going to be all about me. And it was going to involve Medusa mask. Something had to happen, and all I was waiting on was the chance that the something would come from someone else, not from me, like I'd get summoned away or there'd be a fire or Dr. Wilson would move to another neighborhood and take his buddy with him.

None of those things happened. What happened was I had to run some cans of beans or something up to Mrs. Mendez' house for my Aunt, and coming back I saw them again, clearing some brush by the corner of Dr. Wilson's house, and before I knew what I was doing or why, I called out.

"Hey!"

No response.

"Hey! Hey, monster mask!"

I couldn't believe I'd said that, but what else could I call them?

They stopped and turned to me, arms at their sides. Those bird shit eyes weren't looking at me, they were focused on two different, random points, but I knew that there were eyes behind those little slits, and they were on me, walking up to him. Big, massive, solid. Fat over muscle. Totally silent. Not even some breath whistling through the neck hole of the mask, nothing. Didn't move an inch as I came over. Still holding a cut branch in one hand. The air was thick with the smell of fresh-cut brush, sort of resinous, very strong, a little like turpentine.

I came up a few feet away and opened my mouth, but what exactly was I going to ask? I mean, now was the time for me to ask something, but it's like for the first time I realized that asking something would mean actually picking individual words and putting them together to form a clear question. I couldn't just ball up all my confusion and creeps and toss it to Medusa mask to work out for me. What's up with the mask, what's with the mask, why do you always—do you always?—they do—why always you mask wear, why the mask? I couldn't manage to come up with a possible question. It was like asking why someone was in a wheelchair, first thing, right up front. You don't walk up to someone and first thing ask them what the fuck is the matter with them, although you could. I could.

I opened my mouth, and what ended up coming out was:

"What's your name?"

What did I say? *What's your name?*

Without moving, Medusa mask said two words.

"Dog Scream."

The voice that came out from inside the mask was all wrong. It was tinny and flat, like it was coming through a police radio, but it wasn't muffled by the mask. There was nothing about that voice that had been affected by the mask. The voice from inside the mask was not mechanical, but it was flat and tinny—sharp, not muffled but sharp—so that I heard the words crisply, without any possibility of being wrong. And that quick answer in that weird voice yanked my heart up into my mouth. I couldn't think of anything to say. I think I just stared. After a moment, they turned and shoved the branch down into a plastic garbage can, then bent over to tear up more rattling, dry stuff.

I left them there, like that. Ignoring me. I found my way back to my room—luckily my Aunt wasn't around, she was napping or something—and sat down on my bed. My hands were shaking. Maybe he had one of those voice box things you get when you... after throat surgery or...

Does throat surgery make you change your name? To "Dog Scream"?

I sat watching my shaking hands. After a while they started to move on their own. They started packing my crap up. Putting things into a backpack in no order and without reason, but then again, they were just my hands, right? They couldn't think. I had to leave before my Aunt woke up or I would have to talk to her, and then she would know I'd gone crazy right, and she'd worry and be frightened—well she's going to have to worry and be frightened anyway, isn't she? She didn't worry about what's next door. She'll worry about me, though. I have nowhere to go but away so that's where I'm going, and if I can figure out a way back I'll take it, but right now there's two words spoken in a voice that isn't human anymore going through my mind over and over, and each time they repeat it's like a buzzer shaking my whole body, and it's coming from next door, so it's time to go.

I couldn't go back into the street. The sound of brush being rammed into a garbage can told me that. So, I went up the trail again. There's a concrete fire cut further along the ridge that links the trail to the street up by the landfill.

I walked for a long time, down out of the hills. Eventually, I came to the highway, the little three- and four-unit apartment buildings, the liquor store, the candy store. I shoplifted a bottle of water there. Kept walking. Over the hill, past the community college, the gas stations, the row of grandma stores with silk flowers and potpourri. The generic fancy Italian place. Two words behind me, echoing in the hills, getting further away, but still there, smoldering. Just keep going. Two feet, one after another. I don't know anybody.

A rubber mask. There in the window, a row of them. The Halloween store. I go inside. It smells like paint, rubber, plastic, glue in here. A paper top hat covered in gold glitter, a plastic scythe, red devil horns, bags of vampire fangs, a fake rat. I look for a Medusa mask. There it is. Just the same. There's three of them, all on a steel hook. All off the same mold. I don't want to touch them. I don't want to have anything to do with them. I want to run out of here. I want to throw myself in front of a moving car. But not really. My hand reaches out and takes down a monkey mask. It's a monkey, not a chimp. It's not Curious George either. It's a plain, general, no-name monkey, with a serious expression. I put it on. I don't feel better. I feel different. I leave with it on. Maybe nobody noticed. I don't care. I'm walking down the street, which I see framed through the slits under the staring, innocent eyes of the mask. I see the slanting gold of the sunbeams. I see the flowers bob in the breeze, planters full of them. People float past me like drowned bodies. The daytime has flooded the street. It sweeps everything before it, the waters of daytime pushing me along, pushing everyone, watering us with time, pressing on the gleaming glass windows, the glittering gems in the vitrines of the jewelry stores, the sparkling white tiles of an ice cream place, the hoods and windshields of the cars.

I don't know anybody. I never will.

Milking

EVERY MORNING, LUCAS came downstairs, passed through the parlor and the kitchen, and entered the small room at the back of the house to find his glass of milk waiting for him in a saucer on the table, a gleaming white tube in the gloom back there, the sides of the glass peppered with droplets of gemlike condensation. The noise of the surf came in through the thin windowpanes, and, as Lucas took the cool glass in both hands and raised it carefully to his mouth, his father would come in behind him to watch him drink it, perhaps to make certain that he drank all of it. The chill bulk of the milk would shift swallow by swallow from the glass to his belly, vanish into him in a few moments, and he would return the glass, containing nothing now but a settling white film, solemnly to its saucer. Turning around, he would fully enter the benevolent presence of his father, who would settle his blessing hand carefully on the head of his son and smile, his brow contracted. Then mother would join them, taking away the glass and saucer, while father set breakfast on the table for them all.

This small room in the back of the house was square, protruding from the rear of the building like a snub nose, with windows that overlooked the shore. This table stood on one leg, and the chairs surrounding it were all different. Lucas had a fine velvet seat with little pads riveted along the curved back. His father sat on a stool, and his mother had a narrow, high-backed chair with a shallow seat. Taciturn, soft-spoken, gentle, they murmured to each other and to him in voices that were barely audible over the rush of the waves. They ate all their meals in the cramped back room of the house to spare the pristine dining room, which, as far as Lucas could remember, had been exclusively reserved for the purpose of celebrating his birthday. For the remainder of the year, the dining room was merely another room his parents had to keep clean and in good order, almost as if it were possible he might surprise them by having a birthday at any time. Occasionally, he would look in at the door of the dining room to see the pale reflection of the dim light of day glistening against the stacked edges of the plates in the porcelain cabinet and warming the polished wood of the long tabletop.

After breakfast, Lucas usually would sit for a little while in the parlor, perhaps still gazing at the empty space where the piano used to be, wondering what had been wrong with it, waiting for his mother's sister, Aunt Inger, to come by with her own children and see him safely to school. However, it was the winter holiday now, and so Lucas was at liberty to do whatever he liked, provided he didn't leave the radius of his parents' supervision.

"I'm taking Smokey down to the beach," he told his mother. She turned her thin face to him, smiling, her red-rimmed eyes full of love.

"Stay within sight of the house," she said, her voice barely above a whisper.

"I will," he said.

When he entered the kitchen, Smokey was lying in his usual spot, not far from the stove. He was what father called a good-sized dog, but lean, who rose with a little difficulty when Lucas called to him. They left the house, the yard, and walked down to the shore.

The day was misty but not too cold. Looking back, Lucas could see his mother's figure in the window of her bedroom upstairs. Down below, his father stood watching from the kitchen window. The beach was nearly empty, and there was no one nearby. Lucas spent the

morning tossing stones and sticks that Smokey would eventually re-
trieve, dropping them at his feet, then looking around a moment before raising his head, searching blearily until he found the boy's eyes,
then lowering his head again.

Standing on the beach, Lucas saw a vacant, endless world
stretched out on every side. Even the enormous ocean was engulfed
in a haze of mist and spray that collected the particles of his vision
only to disperse them into a glowing white cloud, the vault of nature
that dwarfed the straggling line of houses along the coast and the little
town tucked into a notch in the coastline, a narrow harbor there,
where the mountains veered closer to the water and raised the surrounding land. There again were his parents, tiny figures moving
about a doll's house, bleached and peeling, left out in the sun and rain.

Lucas waited to see if any of his friends, the children who lived in
the neighboring houses, would turn up, but none of them did. This
happened sometimes. Lucas didn't mind being alone with Smokey.
He could always sneak away, go exploring up toward the ruins of the
old pier, but the last time he went out of sight of the house, his parents
had both become so distraught their behavior alarmed him, and their
relief at seeing him again, their sadness, too, buffeted him with quiet
words and cautious gestures, leaving him with an uneasy feeling that
didn't go away for a long time. There was something about their quiet
fussing, their distress, that made him feel as though he'd inflicted a
more lasting kind of harm to them in some way.

After school, one or another of his teenaged cousins would take
care of him while his father was away and his mother was resting, but
now his cousins weren't available, it seemed. Aunt Inger was busy,
too, with holiday things he only vaguely understood, but, when he
came in again, slightly dazed from a glut of space and sea air, she was
there, sitting in the parlor talking with his mother.

"We'll start soon," she told Aunt Inger as he came into the house.

She greeted him warmly, as always, and his mother smiled her close-lipped smile at him.

"Did you have a nice walk?' she asked.

"It's so misty!" he said.

"It is!" Aunt Inger said. "You're right!"

Lucas felt encouraged by this and began speaking. Aunt Inger and his mother listened to a recitation of his observations that day with little cooings of appreciation. When he finished, Aunt Inger said—

"He has the eye of an artist. We should get him a painting set!"

Mother gave her a particular look then, and Aunt Inger added, immediately:

"When the time is right!"

Lucas knew that his parents did not want to spoil him, that this was the meaning of that look, and, since the prospect of receiving a painting set didn't stir him in any way, he didn't wonder about the time. There was, though, an idea too, albeit an inchoate, elusive one, more like an impression, that the concern of his parents mysteriously combined their reluctance to spoil him with the disappearance, one by one, of various things belonging to the family—the piano, the old gilt mirror that used to hang over the mantelpiece, and the porcelain figurines that had been kept with great care on a shelf high on the wall. He had started to believe that, as children grow, their houses become more empty. Growing was an invisible process that converted time into accumulated physical size. There was something plausible, or at least symmetrical, about the idea that there was a balance involved, that nothing came from nothing, and something, like the piano or the mirror, had to be lost in order for him to grow. Everyone, his parents, his teachers, his many relatives, all referred often to his promising future. From time to time, he thought about it, but he really couldn't imagine it; the future, for him, could never be anything but scenes from a story book, rewritten with himself at the center. Lucas was happy as he was. He had no strong desire to change, and very little curiosity about himself. For him, growing was something that was happening to him, not something he was doing. It would happen in any case, nothing would stop it, there was nothing he could do about it, and no reason to care about it. As he outgrew his clothes, they would be replaced with similar, larger versions. Smokey was old; he would die some day, but there would be another dog then, of the same size, who would fill his place in the household. Maybe they would bury him on the beach, under the sand.

Lucas padded up the thickly-carpeted stairs to his room after a few more words with his Aunt, who told him that his cousins would be coming by later for dinner. He received this news ambivalently. What he really wanted to do was to play with imaginary friends, children who weren't there, so that he could enjoy himself without having to be seen or to respond. His mother and his Aunt began whispering together as he went upstairs, which was not strange, and his mind was crossed by the pleasant suspicion that they might be planning some kind of surprise for him.

The enemy emerged from beneath his bed in sinister, deviously-moving ranks, but the vigilant defenders did not fail to notice and repel them. As he played, he heard, from time to time, the faint tinkling of the door chime, followed by muted greetings, sung high or rumbled low. These were his cousins, his uncle, Aunt Inger's friend Lily. As the gloom of the day began to deepen in the late afternoon, he looked up to see his mother gazing fondly at him from the threshold of his bedroom, obscured by the shadow of the open door.

"Come down and say hello to everyone," she said.

They were at the top of the stairs. Lucas could hear the family voice meshed in a subdued music below. He was struck by the almost furtive way everyone spoke and again thought of some nice surprise that might be waiting for him. His mother, then, turned to face him when she was few steps down, the better to fix his eyes with her own.

"Just remember to keep away from the kitchen until we're done in there," she said.

This was a command he was always given on these occasions, and it had a special status. He knew his parents doted on him, and were forgiving to a fault, but this was one of the few iron rules they'd established. Once, when the distinctive creak of the kitchen door caught his attention and he'd gone without thinking to peek inside, his father had stepped in front of him, springing up like a mythological soldier, to bar his way.

"Go read with your Auntie Inger," he'd said. He spoke in the even tone that he always used, but there was a startled look in his eye that Lucas did not fail to notice, although he didn't comprehend it. His friends, however, had all told him about inexplicably firm rules in their families, and even arbitrary commands, so he assumed this was one of those adult secrets that he would come to understand in time.

"I will," he told his father.

They welcomed him on sight, in their mild way. Seeing them now in the light of the lamps, which had already been lit, both his parents looked nervous, bright-eyed, flushed pink, self-conscious. Aunt Inger looked like that too. So did his cousins. It was something that would have been easier to miss if they weren't all together in one place. Lucas wondered about their strange, lingering sadness—but it couldn't be real sadness, even if they kept their voices down like people who didn't want to wake a sleeping baby in the next room. Their manner reminded him, come to think of it, of people with newborn babies in the house; they had the same odd combination of fatigue and alertness. What was it? They were all overwhelmed with adult business. That's the way it is. He felt more grown-up for thinking about it that way, closer to his parents and relatives, and a mimicry of resignation passed over him as a novel and interesting experience.

Lucas greeted everyone, and then Aunt Inger led him across the hall to the sewing room. The light was better there. Together they sat on the stiff horsehair sofa, she reading to him, and he looking at the illustrations and following the tip of her tapering finger as it scanned the lines of text. This was one of his favorite books. He knew the story by heart and took satisfaction in the way the events slotted reliably into place, one after another. As she read, he could hear the bustle of preparations going on in the house, the regular squeak of the kitchen door, the tramp of feet, the incessant murmur. After a while, his father appeared in the door, summoning Aunt Inger to assist his mother with the last preparations. He looked haggard, but then helping to make family dinner always seemed to tax him, and he didn't fail to give his son an encouraging smile.

"Are you hungry?" he asked.

"Oh yes!" Lucas said.

His father laughed inaudibly.

"We'll begin in a minute," he said, going away with Aunt Inger.

Lucas went to the bathroom in the meantime, then made his way through the back of the house toward the parlor, where he could hear the clank of plates and plink of steel forks and spoons. They didn't use the silver anymore.

The door was open, the kitchen was in its usual order, redolent now of onions and chicken, and there was another, unfamiliar smell too. There was something unusual about the kitchen, he realized: the door in the corner, what they called the closet door, and which was supposed to be impossible to open for some reason, was ajar. He'd never seen inside. And his parents had told him clearly that the door was useless. Had they been hiding something from him? Or had they only just managed to get it open?

He slipped across the kitchen and, making sure no one was coming, peeked in. The next moment he heard the tread of what was almost certainly his mother coming up behind him and he impulsively slipped into the closet, pulling the door back to where it was.

"I'll just get the bowls," his mother was saying.

The bowls were kept in cupboards on the far side of the kitchen. If she were only retrieving them and bringing them out to the table in the parlor – not the dining room – then he could duck out of the closet unnoticed when she left again in a few moments. He couldn't be sure he was doing anything his parents wouldn't permit him to do.

The odd smell was much stronger in the closet, which was, he now saw, actually a small room, completely bare except for a plain wooden table situated directly beneath a skylight. And the room smelt. He'd never smelled anything like it; it was a gamey smell, not meat, not like a butcher's shop, not quite, but a little like that, and maybe just a little like the smell of sweat, freshly sweated? There was a trace of pungency, too, a little like stagnant sea water. He couldn't connect this disgusting smell with anything he'd encountered before in the house, but at the same time it wasn't really unfamiliar, was it? Where did it come from? It was everywhere in the room, equally strong; it was just the smell of the room itself.

He heard the clatter of bowls as his mother gathered them. Moving quietly, he went over to the table. There were no drawers, nothing. Did they reserve this room only to store this one table? He looked beneath the table and found nothing there except what might have been some scuff marks in the thin dust on the floor; as he looked, he kept his balance by pressing his hand and forearm against the top of the table, and he noticed then that the wood was warm. He drew his palm over the top and found it was nearly all uniformly warm, as if a big basin of hot water had been left there for a while. Near the far corner to him, he spotted a splash of milk. Was this where they kept the milk they gave him each morning? Were they all out? Was that why there was nothing in this room but this table? Did they pour out a bowl of warm milk in here? Was it milk he was smelling?

Maybe—he thought with a little rush of pleasure at figuring out a plausible explanation for this enigma—they were making cheese in here, and he would find it waiting for him on the table.

His mother was hurrying back to the parlor, most likely with an armful of bowls, and so he slipped out of the closet, or little room, carefully replacing the door as it was, and then darted out into the hall so that he could enter the parlor through the door closer to the sewing room, and fool everyone into thinking he'd come from there. When he entered, the same faint cheer that had rose to meet him earlier was repeated, and he took his place, suppressing a thrill at the thought that his ruse had worked, that his trespass would not be noticed. Then came a flash of alarm at the thought of the dusty floor, the possibility that he'd left tracks in it – but no, he would have seen their tracks too, wouldn't he? It was clear they were using the room, that they had been misleading him about it; hadn't the door swung on its hinges easily? Wouldn't they be ... fused, that's it, rusted shut, if the door hadn't been used in such a long time?

Maybe they put Smokey in there sometimes? Was it Smokey he'd been smelling? Was there something wrong with him, that they were keeping from him, that they had to treat in secret? Smokey was old, but he seemed well enough. He never smelled like that, even when he'd doused himself in the ocean. That wasn't the answer.

Sitting on all manner of chairs, filling their plates with the food on the coffee table and then perching them on the crowded little side tables, they all ate together, talking merrily in their hushed way. His cousins were giddy, like people who were so tired they were starting to find it funny, and Aunt Inger knocked over a wine glass with a clumsiness that wasn't like her at all. They were all drinking very freely, and even his parents, while they were more restrained than the others, still tossed back glass after glass. Smokey munched food from his bowl by the fireplace. Lucas looked surreptitiously for a cheese dish. The smell of the little room was here in the parlor too now, but so faint he wondered if it weren't clinging to his own clothes. There was no clear source for it. The smell was simply there, like the watery twilight filtering through the faded dimity curtains, and mingled with the vinous smell of drinking, the savory onion smell of their dinner.

Everyone was kind to Lucas and made a point of saying something to him. When the meal was over, the adults rearranged the parlor for coffee, and the younger cousins took charge of Lucas and played a board game with him in the sewing room.

When everyone had departed for the night, his parents cleared up, sighing and agitated with nervous fatigue that made them a little curt with each other. Lucas found himself in the kitchen with his mother, but she simply gave him a feeble smile and continued cleaning up. His father entered a moment later, greeted Lucas in passing, and helped his mother. The door to the little room was closed.

"Did you enjoy dinner?" his father asked him.

Lucas nodded. He wondered if he could ask them about the little room without giving them any reason to think he'd looked inside, and perhaps to impose on them the idea that he had not done what he had done. Why would he ask if he had already seen? So, the question would be kind of a lie. But then, hadn't they lied to him about that door being stuck?

Lucas didn't find himself asking them anything and went up to bed when his father told him to, as usual. Everything had been as usual, with the one exception of his discovery of that room whose emptiness would not leave him alone. Lying in bed that night, he imagined the table standing downstairs, confined to that room like an animal in a cage. Now the table was beginning to walk on its stiff wooden legs. He could hear the wooden feet rap against the ground like tiny hooves. It strained upward toward the dim glow of the clouded skylight, and began to call out in a high, rasping voice, the noise that a table makes when it is dragged across bare floorboards. Left alone at night, it was calling, its voice ringing in the confines of the small room, panting, and bumping against the door. Sometimes it was as if he were in the room too, and other times he saw himself, the bed, and down through the transparent house to the darkened room, the table shining in its outlines but eclipsed by the darkness, moving unnaturally.

There was a squeal of wood downstairs. This persistent but irregular noise drew him back into shallower sleep until he finally came fully awake. Lucas listened in the dark. He could hear the waves rushing on the beach, and something outside rattling in the wind, and, then, the kitchen door.

"If I hear it again, then I'm not imagining it," he told himself.

He was nearly asleep again when the noise was repeated.

"I did hear it. I think. I did hear it... So, if I hear it again, then … something's happening."

When he heard the squeal again, he felt a flash of irritation.

"It's *nighttime*," he thought, meaning that it didn't seem fair to him that he should have to go to bed and be quiet if other people were not required to do the same. Or were his parents making something for him in the kitchen, a nice surprise? That surprise he'd expected during the day, and that hadn't happened – was it about to happen soon?

He probed the soft nullity around him with his hearing, and, without discovering anything definite, he did become aware of action in the night, in the house, down there. Like a low rumble, more felt than heard. Lucas wanted to know what was going on, if only so that he could stop thinking about it and get back to sleep. Smokey lay in his nest at the foot of the bed, asleep, very still. The noise didn't faze him, or even wake him.

As the top of the stairs came into view, he saw a faint illumination sifting up from below, throwing the railing into dim relief against the darkness. Padding down the steps, he saw that the glow shone from the small gap beneath the kitchen door, making it a livid stripe with a powdery halo. A hushed voice sounded briefly on the other side. If he crept through the dining room he could come around and see into the kitchen without having to open the door; he would be able to see the surprise without being seen, without their knowing he was there.

It was only just a moment before he turned the corner that the odor struck him again. Sharp, rancid, and bitter, like stale sea water. It wasn't a composite smell, that was what bothered him about it, not just that it was bad, but that it was the smell of some special bad thing, not a chance mixing of smells.

They were all there, as if they hadn't left at all, but had only concealed themselves in the house until he'd gone to sleep. They stood in the light of a lantern that blazed with the transparent glare of a very pure and dazzling light that burned a blue-black flaw into his vision, forcing him to blink and look down. In the glare of that pale light he had seen them all congregated around the wide-open door to the little room; someone he couldn't make out for the brilliancy of the lamp was directing its beams over the threshold, and everyone was waiting, leaning, looking in. He was reminded of pictures he'd seen of surgical operations in books.

There was a long inhalation inside the little room. Someone in there was breathing in and in and in, quietly, but so that the room hummed, like a wooden lung. Everyone in the room shifted in reaction to what they were seeing, and Lucas heard a voice from the table inside that could have belonged to either his father or his mother give a long shuddering groan, the prayer of a suffering animal, and there was lapping, and motion, a releasing of bated breath, and a pressing toward the door, and from hand to hand he saw a tall, clean, empty glass was being passed forward. When the groan came again, louder, barely stifled and more insistent, Lucas staggered, ran, threw himself out the back door and into the wind and spray of the beach at night, losing himself at once in the gusts of icy mist.

Lucas ran until the boiling black and white line of the waves repelled him too, causing him to turn and struggle through the sand along the shore. When he stopped, and turned, the blank contour of the house was not that far behind him, as inscrutable as any. It was constantly at risk in his vision of sliding into the shapeless mass of the other houses. Lucas' knees buckled. He collapsed on the sand, and the cold made the tears on his face burn like slashes. His head drooped and swam, his face bunched and hot, his nose running, and he knew he didn't have the strength to throw himself into the black and white ocean, which would snatch up, toss, and smash him against the beach. Tomorrow morning exploded with terror. He would stand as ever in front of a tall gemmed glass of white milk, with the eyes of his father and the weight of everything in life thundering down on top of him without a sound.

His hands spread out and traveled over the sand, picking at stones, bits of seaweed, cigarette butts, until he found a pebble that looked right, lifted it, and his eyes caught the gleam of a fragment of broken glass that he picked up instead. Lucas bared his left arm and held the glass edge over its clean skin, shaking with terror in the icy mist. It took him a long time. After a moment, he watched a thin ribbon of amazing red fall across his arm and drip into the sand, forming a little dark patch that grew bit by bit, and then stopped. Lucas dropped the glass and studied his arm, examining his red wound, the first of many.

Stillville

I DIDN'T WANT to think of it as "stillville," but the name forced itself on me. I found a little house and started living here. Even though I worked a town away, I chose to live here. Even though the house was more expensive and less convenient than an apartment near my place of work would have been, I chose the expense and the trouble. The price had not been especially high, but it was dear at my income. The house was not entirely sound when I bought it either. I knew nothing of home repair at the time. Living here compelled me to learn. I patched up the leaks in the roof. I replaced the windows in the back. I had to tear everything out of the backyard. For a time, it wasn't clear whether or not I could keep the garage. In the end, I did. It's standing out there now. I can see it through the rear window. When I turn my head, I can see the street out the front window. There's the house across the street, the tree, the parked station wagon, centered between the mailbox on one side and the driveway cut on the other side. It's as reliable as a painted mural. Above the street, the daytime sky alternates with the nighttime sky, and clear skies alternate with cloudy skies. Lights are turned on and off, but otherwise the scene is the same. Sometimes the station wagon is gone, sometimes there are no leaves on the tree. The stillness that brought me here never wavers, though. When I go to work, driving into that other town, I can see right away that the buildings and streets, parked cars and trees, aren't really still. They aren't incapable of motion. They only withhold their motion. They are trembling coils, poised with the momentary immobility of a snake about to strike. There's no peace in that merely temporary motionlessness, any more than there is in the brief pause before the roller coaster drops down its incline. The town I work in vibrates incessantly, especially at quitting time. Then everyone is rushing to change into another self and wring a little pleasure from life. People hurry themselves along like their own slave drivers, laying in supplies for the weekend. Pedestrians spray from the buildings like bullets. The clock fires its artillery over the rooftops. The tension varies over these volleys of hours without ever slackening. I've never visited that town at night, but I doubt it would be much different then. I imagine the wary unserenity of the street where I work under a blue night sky. The buildings would look like howling faces and glassy headstones.

My town at noon is quieter than that town would be at four in the morning, I'm sure. Moving here, for all the difficulties that it entailed, was exactly what I wanted. Nothing is ever going to happen to me here.

Something *is* happening to me. I'm becoming more still. I'm undergoing the phases. Outwardly, just like everyone else here, I move. Of course, I move. The stillness is within. It grows inside me here, the same way it has for everyone else. It's active and in motion. All that activity and motion, though, arises from it and subsides back into it. There's no tension at all. There's no sense of lying in wait, no ambush. No waiting, really. It would be more accurate to say, everything becomes a form of waiting. No one here is trying to keep still. It's not something that can be accomplished. I can see there's something off about the idea that I would fixate on being still and then become still, because that would mean moving into a state of motionlessness, which makes no sense. The idea is the reverse. I have to stop moving, which means going with the flow, the silent flows, the flows of silence. Then I will be safe, right in the heart of the vaster current of time, carried along, motionless. No more learning. No need for concern. Asking for nothing to happen is like slamming on the brakes on a busy highway. If I really want nothing to happen, I have to siphon into one of the many eddies in the ribbon of events. Then I could glide friction-lessly from each instant to the next, let them mesh and blur into one perennial, muted outpouring of fraught color and jangled, senseless noise. Even all the trouble I had to take fixing up my house, wrangling with the bank, which was situated in the same town, was less and less disturbing. It was as if patching up the house were bringing it into closer accord with its surroundings. I had to see my house from the perspective of the town as a whole in order to integrate it, which made me a sort of unwitting agent for the town. This required a realignment of my thoughts, too. It would be more accurate to say that I had to change my way of thinking. My house was part of the bank of a river of quiet. My repairs were made slowly and with as little noise as pos-sible. After I'd finished, the house looked no different, inside or out. It was important that it be unchanged on the inside, because this isn't a question of superficial appearances. "stillville" isn't quiet because people keep their dirty secrets well hidden, but because there are no secrets here. There are no hiding places or reasons to use them, unless the whole town could be considered a hiding place.

Leaving town, going to work, is more and more like driving into a war zone. And yet, as my days lengthen in "stillville," this war affects me less, steadily less. Lately, I've simply found myself at work. I went there without noticing it. The tedium and frustration of my commute is gone. At work, I do my tasks easily, regularly. Once I suffered for this job. I created patterns of work, which helped to ensure that I didn't overlook anything or miss deadlines. Unexpected changes would keep cropping up and disrupting these patterns, inducing a fierce distress in me that seems disproportionate now. After I'd been living in my new home for a while, I began to wonder if we were enjoying a period of greater regularity, with fewer surprises. Or, actually, no surprises. In a spirit of idle curiosity, I reviewed my calendar. To my surprise, I realized that the last few weeks had been as chaotic as any I'd experienced during my time with the company. By my count, more than half the events in it were struck through with long, steady pen-strokes and rescheduled with neat arrows. I could only marvel at my progress. My progress in slowing down my progress. Days that, at one time, would have wrung me out, would have had me raving to no one in my car as I drove to and from work, and left me fuming as I lay down to stare at the ceiling at night in lieu of sleeping, had passed me by in silence.

No more of that. Less and less, and then no more. I carry the quiet, without magic, or any effort, everywhere I go. I neither acknowledge nor avoid my neighbors. I am aware of them, as I'm sure they are aware of me. We grow in awareness of each other. This awareness depends on our being still. When I sit in my living room, I am aware of my neighbors all around me, sitting in their living rooms. When I pad silently upstairs to my narrow bed and lie down, I am aware of them lying on their narrow beds around me, like so many figures hovering in space, all the same distance above the ground. Those of us on this side of the block sleep with our feet to the east, and those of us on the other side of the block sleep with their feet to the west. Between the rows of our sleeping heads, there is a sloping gulf, like the fold between the pages of an open book. Each of us is a sentence, complete on its own line. The war goes on without us, somewhere else. It is not here. It is not in us.

Together, we join in a stillness that is greater than the sum of us, to which we have given a life of its own. It is our helper. We all want to join as closely as possible to it. Perhaps this is why we don't see each other or speak to each other. We do speak, and see, but we do it at a certain angle to each other. It's not quite a matter of keeping up appearances. After all, who are we appearing to? It might just be the last vestiges of an old habit. It could also be a little favor we do each other, giving each other the slightest nudge only so that we can turn with a quiet pleasure back to our own silence again. I think, though, that we do it primarily to reassure each other that our silence is not the kind that masks resentment or signals it.

Perhaps one day I will quit my job and remain here all the time. I think I would like that, but the power of this peace is strong. I don't need to quit my job, remain here all the time, because the peace is inside me. It is me. Not enough, but more and more. Is it that I want to live my life in a dream? I think what I want is to live without knowing or feeling it. I don't want to die. I know for a virtual certainty that none of us do. If you want to die, you die, you don't move here. You move here because you want to live without knowing it. You aren't looking to live some dream or other, an adventure of glorious sex and righteous violence. You want to live in a dreamy way, absently, wandering without being lost. You want to be a dream instead of being yourself. The dream I am becoming is not a dream of anything. In the dream I am becoming, the streets are the same, the houses, the people, the sky, my body, are all the same. The events of the day are the same. So, what's the difference? Time. It passes through me now. I'm becoming a perfect filter for time. It passes through me, and nothing clings. There's no trace of it. Nothing of me clings to it, either; nothing of me is borne away, nothing of me washes downstream, lodges on the bank. No one downstream knows I am upstream. I'm moving into the future without touching it, like a spaceman walking on nothing in outer space.

"Oh my God!"

Your voice shook me like thunder. Suddenly I was awake, at work, blinking, and my hand—my hand was on fire. You were there, shock on your face.

I tried to review what had happened. I was in the little kitchen area at the office. I had been reaching for a paper cup. Someone had placed a coffee mug with a broken handle on the shelf beside the bundle of paper cups. I had mistaken where my hand should go, and the jagged end of the mug's broken handle had gashed the top of my hand. I stared down at the unbelievable blood, the redness, and nothing was muffled. You were there. You had been working with me for months, and I never paid you any particular attention before. Now you were sympathetically helping me, leading me unresisting into the women's bathroom, with some words of warning as we came in. That was where the first aid kit was kept, and you knew that. You washed my hand.

"Let me wrap it for you," you said.

You bound up the wound. It was your alarm, your compassion, the pain you felt on my behalf, that startled me out of my dream. That was why I noticed my pain. The pain was unpleasant, of course, but you saved me from obliviously walking around the office with blood dripping from my hand. As I imagined this, I had to imagine also the upset and confusion that would have created. No one just walks around dripping blood, that's true. I would have smeared it on the paperwork. There would have been questions. The prospect of answering questions shouldn't have alarmed me, but it did, in fact, the idea alone frightened me, quickened me, sent adrenaline to my stomach. I was awake again, in the old way, in the middle of the workday, afraid, in pain—but you were there, looking me in the eye with stunning compassion. You were what woke me up, not the pain or the fear.

"You look a little *green*," you said. "Maybe you should go home."

The idea that you would suggest that to me was almost funny. I smiled. As I smiled, I realized that I had been smiling at work in the usual way, at appropriate times, but that this smile was different because you were making me do it. No particular individual had made me smile in a long time; I had been smiling, when I smiled, because the general circumstances warranted a smile. But this time, I smiled because you compelled me to. How? Your actions made your warmth palpable to me. The warmth stayed in me after you had gone back to your desk. I could feel the smile lingering on my face, and I wanted to sniff the air in order to get a clearer impression of the fragrance that you were wearing that day. I found I liked it. But driving back home was more painful than it had been in months; I drove home feeling like a man being hounded by a pack of wolves. When I pulled into my driveway, I nearly failed to park the car in the usual way, and, when I had parked, I still had to sit at the wheel for a while before I could muster the willpower to get out. The sound of my breathing filled the car. I thought I might cloud the windows over. I wondered if the others were aware of that. When I finally did manage to get inside, everything about my house leapt out at me, and for a moment I was almost uncertain whether or not I had entered a stranger's house by mistake. Your face was somehow at work. Your look of compassion had taken me. Your fragrance—was I still smelling it, even here? Was it on my hand? No, but my hand still smelled like the soap in the woman's washroom, which you had used to clean it. I saw the white tile, the fluorescent light, the gleaming steel fixtures, the mirror, and you, a dark presence, dabbing my hand with a paper towel, transferring your gaze now from it to my face. Your eyes, full of compassion, haunting compassion, were like images of another planet.

Once I'd seen them I couldn't—

I saw them, I kept —

While I'm driving home—I saw them see me —

Your bandage on my hand. Whenever it came into view, the sight of it startled me so much I had to suppress an impulse to slam on the brakes or swerve off the road. I tore off the bandage and threw it out the window.

When I crossed the town line, as usual I could feel the car pressing into the bank of silence, but there was a knot of something humming inside me. I parked. I walked up the flat paving stones to my front door in silence, with the long shadows of the passing day lying all around me on the ground, draped over my walls and my roof. I went inside and replaced my work clothes with my after-work clothes. My living room was like a kiln of emptiness. I sat in it, trying not to fill, but your eyes —

I looked down at my torn hand. My vision swam.

From that day, I was afraid to see you again. *You* didn't frighten me. Something had gone out of line in me when I saw your eyes, though, because your eyes could never see things my way—you could join me in silence, but not in *that* silence. That silence was the domain of only solitary people. Even that isn't right; it isn't a landscape of isolated people, but an empty landscape, empty even of me; where there is a presence, but only as one, the pronoun "one."

Just the other day, I wouldn't have been able to refer to my heart without smiling. I mean, smiling with derision. The idea that I had "a heart," which was—was it only yesterday?—such a quaint and comical thing to think, was now the only thing, the only problem.

Driving in my car, I found myself litanizing your flaws, whatever I could think of—and it was all nonsense. I was someone who had preferred not to have preferences. How could I identify flaws? I knew you weren't perfect, but this was only abstract. We all know not to think in terms of perfection. And what was the point of trying to reason with something that had nothing to do with reason, and what was reason to me or me to reason? If I said a word to you about—it would make—

I only want to say numbly ordinary things to you and make no difference. I litanized you, thinking foolishly that I would find flaws and somehow talk myself out of—it was just one more way to think about you, and it only further provoked that quickening something inside me—my heart.

If I said a word to you it would make—things—real, too real—

I'd be—more than exposed—I'd be concrete, all too real myself—

But I'm old! I'm old, I know how these things end, and they always end. Now things are beginning. It doesn't make sense. It doesn't make sense that things should begin. Especially not now, when I've put myself past the point of any beginning. The point of no starting is behind me, but things are starting anyway. It's as if I'd failed. My will to stop wasn't really pure.

You spoke to me. Out of nowhere, you appeared—it was in the hallway, I was heading for the entrance. I was going for ... for lunch, I think. You asked me about my hand, if it was better, and before I knew what I was doing you had me in your eyes again, that same compassion that rang through me, harder than if you'd punched me. I told you it was all right, and I thanked you, but I wasn't professional. I stammered, fumbling for the words when the words were "thank you"—just "thank you." You smiled without a trace of condescension. You wished me well, that's what you said. What now? You had gone on, and I was going on, in the same direction. You asked me about my department, about my work. I found myself asking you mirroring questions about your department, your work. You said something about a deadline, and I found it funny, and laughed. You laughed with me. I parted from you at the end of the hall in a state of confusion. I didn't know what to do with myself. I had to grope in my mind for the old habits, which I thought were set in me, set in concrete with bars, and which I couldn't now even start to remember. They were on the other side of a gossamer-thin barrier all of a sudden, and I had to try before they would begin again. I spent the day working and, when I left, I was unsatisfied, as though I had done my work badly. I reviewed my work, mentally, sitting in my parked car, and I couldn't tell if I had done anything wrong. Everything that I was supposed to do had been done. I'd missed no deadlines. The only thing—everything I did—I did distracted by your eyes, and now your laugh, and that brief conversation. I'd dragged that along with me into everything, so that for a moment I had an impulse to rush back to the office and check to see if I hadn't been unwittingly writing nothing but transcripts of what we said to each other, and descriptions of your behavior, rather than what I'd been ordered to write. I knew, though, that I hadn't, or at least, that nothing of that encounter had made it into the words I'd written. But some of the words I'd written, as part of what I had been ordered to write, were words you had used, that was the thing. It was as though your words were coming back to me in my own writing, not just the same words, but somehow, now, when I wrote them. What am I saying? They were specifically yours now, just because I'd heard you speak them, addressed to me. Words as common as "department" and "deadline" and "office" and "thank you."

An entire conversation, over the better part of an hour, this time. I can't remember a word, it all happened so quickly, and took such a long time. You said you thought you were a little sick of your usual spot, and that you wanted to give this place a try, and you asked me what was good there. Of course, I never ordered anything different. I found myself speaking to you, and you listened, holding me with your eyes, as I said things to you, ordinary enough things, and I was not voluble at all, but something inside me was going wild. It wanted to talk forever if only you would listen.

I never dream, but that night I dreamed I was driving through stillville, and sometimes flying along the ground without a car, more and more without a car, and watching as the houses and trees, street signs and silent corners, its dim blocks and vacant intersections, all faded into the gloom as I went by. It was like the planet was rolling out from under me in silence, disappearing without a struggle, vanishing sorrowfully. The sadness was so intense I sat up in bed, clutching my chest, gasping, and burst into tears.

I realized that I was going to say something to you the next time I saw you. It was as if a voice had said —

"It's going to happen."

I felt my hands turn to ice, and my temples began to pound.

"It's going to happen."

I was sitting in my living room, vacancy churning all around me, and I couldn't sit still. Something grabbed my right hand and wrung it out hard—my left hand. I stared at my hands, the one kneading the other, and for a moment I thought I would burst into tears again. I stood and went to the window. I saw the street, everything in its accustomed place, and, over the roof of the house opposite, I could see the remoter lights of the main street shining up into the murk, like fixed and impassive stars. So then, I called on the stillness, and asked it to still *you*.

I turned from the window feeling hollow again, but uncertain, agitated, not knowing what I'd done. There was nothing else I could do, or could have done; I released myself, followed the pattern, went to bed. What's done is done. Although I had no reason to expect it, I did sleep. I awoke a little before dawn. For the first time, I saw the sun come up over the town, and it was only this gradual intensification of light that gave any indication that a new day had begun. I wondered if the town had somehow miraculously depopulated during the night, leaving me inexplicably alone. Nothing stirred. There was certainly no dawn chorus, no whir of traffic. No sound at all, not even wind. What's done is done. I had the impulse to clap my hands, or to make some other sudden noise, just in case I had mysteriously gone deaf overnight, but I stifled it at once. It wasn't for me to break the quiet. Besides, I had heard the faint noises my feet made on the floor, the indistinct clicks and taps of plates and cups as I must have eaten something. I wasn't hungry, and there was a sort of taste, or perhaps only a texture, in my mouth, that suggested I'd eaten. I looked at the clock. Time to go to work. What's done is done.

I drove into work feeling a little sick. My hands and feet went cold at once. I maneuvered the car through traffic in the usual way, changing lanes in all the same spots, at the same times, by the clock. As I made my way along surface streets, my nerves went wild. As I entered the building, I was seized by an impulse to run, to cry aloud, that took a moment or two to suppress. Confronted by the elevator, I struggled to swallow, and I couldn't look up, so when I saw you, I saw you, at first, without seeing your face, which came a moment later. Then I saw your face, as you passed me without a word. There was no sign of recognition there. Nothing familiar. You had the face of a stranger once more, and your eyes were not special any more.

So, then one knew. One worked. One conducted oneself appropriately and worked efficiently. The numbers on the clock went through the regular phases of their daily variations. Then the day ended, and one went home.

My Hand of Glory

T HE BEST CHRISTMAS gift I ever received was my hand of glory. I found it mixed in with the other presents, unlabeled, unwrapped, unadorned, taped-up loose, sliding back and forth in a battered cardboard box beneath the tree in the park. I opened it right there and then, on Christmas Day, and I knew immediately what it was... It still had all its nails and was distinctly corded across the back with tendons; bone dry and discolored—as though it had been baked in an oven. I didn't dare touch it at first. I brought it home still in its box, tucked beneath my overcoat. No one noticed me. Plenty of people walk around hiding things at Christmas.

In my room, at my desk, I opened the box and stared at it again. The thumb was nearly as long as the other fingers. There were no scars. There was no ring. No candle, or wax dripping. The bones of the wrist were splintered, jagged where the hand had been hacked away. There was a rustic elegance about it. And a power. There were times I worried it couldn't be entirely concealed in its box. Those long clever fingers must have played something — piano, or guitar perhaps. I could imagine them nimbly stitching up a seam or folding origami. There was, at most, only the barest suggestion of the odor of decay; more decay; more noticeable by far was a spicy smell, like black pepper. A distinguished smell, that made me think of snuffed candle wicks or freshly-sharpened pencils. When my awe had subsided enough to allow me to touch it, I felt a cold current of old electricity go through me, like the charge from an antique battery. As if electricity could feel old. I turned the hand of glory over, carefully studying the palm. Even stretched like a drumhead, it was deeply engraved with long creases. When I looked more closely, I seemed to see the whorls of the skin's grain shaping astrological and occult symbols that vanished the moment I traced them, although I knew they had only disappeared from view, that they remained unseen. There were callouses at the base of middle and ring fingers, and perhaps that smudge at the base of the little finger was another. Lying on its back, fingers stiffly extended, the open hand—far from forbidding me, the way an upraised hand would—welcomed and even accommodated me.

It was my hand of glory, I could tell. I alone had been allowed to find it. How many others had passed by that tree and failed to see it, before I came? And I found it right away. It was the first thing I saw beneath the tree, and what had there been to see but an old box? Who but me would have bothered to take it up and look inside? There was no doubt at all that the hand of glory had to be mine. Who gave it to me, though? Perhaps it gave itself to me... So, it's not necessary to thank anyone else. The secrecy was another gift. Not a word to Mack about it. Not a word to Cousin Doris. Not a word to anyone.

That night—it had to have been that night—was the first of the... new nights for me, when I first learned what sleep really is. I was sleeping the deepest sleep of my life. I'd be gone, completely gone, the moment my head hit the pillow, no matter how my thoughts had been racing just a moment before. I found myself hurrying, rushing to think about all the things I had to think about before I got into bed, because I knew there would be no more thinking the moment I lay down. And, bear in mind, this is me I'm talking about—I used to lie awake for hours before sliding into an unsatisfying, shallow doze that broke and resettled, broke again over and over, all throughout the night, so that I never did get more than a quarter of an hour's actual rest at a time. A dozen times each night, I would twitch myself awake, stir, turn, groan, and hear my own voice return to me, weirdly changed, from the wall.

But in the new night, falling asleep was really like falling. Practically in the same moment I lay down on my bed, I would be released, falling asleep at once, and falling all night long.

So, even though my life was, in every way, the same empty farce, the same drudgery, the same loneliness it had always been, and Mack was Mack, cousin Doris was still the same, I was waking up each morning refreshed and even lively, with a spring in my step, a certain lust for life. It had to be my hand of glory. Sometimes, when I woke up, I would find myself standing already at my desk, the box open in front of me, my fingers outstretched, brushing the dry tendons, the ridges of skin pleached up at the joints. If I turned from it to face my day, I did it unwillingly, it's true, but with a harder, more valiant core inside me all the same. The hand of glory picked me. I just couldn't forget it. Some people noticed a change, I'm sure, but what did it matter to them whether or not I changed? At the end of the day, when it seemed as though I should feel defeated, I would open the box and brush the hand of glory with my fingers, and something like a dim foreshadowing of ecstasy would sometimes flicker up in me, as if my heart had turned to solid gold.

It was first thing New Year's Day when I woke up feeling something in the bed with me. It was soft and chilled, down by my left foot. I reached down to grab it, see what it was, but somehow, I couldn't find it, couldn't feel anything down there but the weight of the sheet and the cover. Finally I had to turn in my narrow bed to snatch it, thinking that maybe a mouse or something had died in there with me, but my left hand was what my right hand was holding when I brought it back up from beside my feet.

My left hand had come off by itself, during the night, and floated down toward the foot of the bed, falling with me as I fell through sleep, but not attached to me anymore. It was cold and limp, and the thought of it, my numb own fingers brushing my foot as I slept, sent a crushing wave of nausea through me. I flung the thing away. I couldn't bring myself to look at the stump at the end of my arm—I knew it would be raw, red tissue, inflamed and weeping, with the bones protruding like glistening white molars. Bile gushed in my throat, and I slid off the bed and checked the linen for signs of blood, but there was only a little damp spot, down by where my waist had been—such a small spot, it didn't seem likely that the prodigious amount of blood I must have lost would have dried so quickly or left so little trace, and the fluid there didn't smell like blood at all. It might have been saliva, I guess. Perhaps the stump dripped saliva?

I turned, and my eyes fell, of course, on the box. It sat in the center of my desk, even though I had put it away in its usual hiding place the night before. I didn't need to think about it. For once in my pitiful life, I knew exactly what I was doing. It was necessary to do it in one decisive movement—right now. Even a moment's delay would show a lack of faith, and I could lose it all. So I went directly to the box, opened it, pulled out my hand of glory, removing it from the box for the first time, and now I knew why I'd been so careful to keep it virgin, keep it in the box until now, so that its powers would not be in the least dispersed until it was ready, because this was something that had to happen, and that had always had to happen, and I pressed the severed end of the ragged, leathery wrist to the numb and raw stump of my left arm, hearing my left hand flop on the floor behind me in an impotent protest. My eyes were shut hard, streaming with tears. There was no pain, but I felt an explosion of fiery itching that made me bark and leap in place, strangling my sobs as best I could. The echoes of my voice in the silent room came back to me like the noises an animal might make in pain.

Time was passing. I had to open my eyes. What was done was done. But irrevocable things aren't easy to look at, even when you've chosen them. When at last I did open my eyes, lower my head, and raise my arm, I felt a smile parting the curtain of tears that were already drying on my face—never to fall again! no, never again!

My hand of glory is clever; already it perfectly mimicked my natural hand. It was still long, dry, cold, but the trenches between the bones had filled, and every moment its color was more and more the color of my right hand. Soon it was an even better, more plausible, and more vivid color than my right hand could manage. Once upon a time, the left hand had been reserved for baser tasks. But for me, from now on my right hand would handle the banalities of life. My hand of glory was ascendant now. Now things really would be different. I could have laughed right in Mack's face when I saw him—really, it was only the power of the hand that gave me the strength to contain myself. *Happy New Year!* I nearly bayed it in his face, like a mad dog, wild with hilarious vindication after ripping itself free from its chain.

What was it like, the first time I touched something with my hand of glory? I can't recall what it was I touched first, although I suppose I was very careful to choose something auspicious. The sensation took my breath away and left me gasping as if my chest were being squeezed in a vice. It wanted to be alone and swinging freely by my side, although I could just stand having it in my jacket or trouser pocket, if not for too long. It felt at once too much and too little. Texture, pressure, temperature, all in the abstract, in comparison with the unremarkable and ordinary sensations transmitted to me by my quotidian right hand. If I were to place it on the desk in front of me, for example, I would feel a tactile version of an image of the grain of the wood, and the feeble warmth of the desk lamp that shone on it would register to my nerves as a sort of patina, finely granulated and measured out in an exact number, unknown to me, but not entirely. The fingers opened and closed as usual, the hand moved on the wrist, which still itched maddeningly where the flesh had knitted together so precisely there was no mark at all, no sign of any kind that any graft had taken place. But even then, the motion was also abstract. Each movement of each digit had a distinct character and numerical regularity, or I should say a geometrical aspect, I couldn't understand, couldn't rationally fathom, but which I could feel as plainly as I might say "that's the color orange" or "this chicken is salty." My hand of glory inscribed its geometrical designs for itself, or for someone, to see, or not yet, directly into space, etched them there with every motion it made, even as it hung from the end of my arm, and I passed from place to place. With greater understanding and keener vision through the darkness of everyday life I perhaps will one day see those lines and read those angles and figures as readily as I do written words now.

It still makes me smile, when I remember how terribly terribly careful I was with my hand of glory at first. It still makes me smile...

I kept it in my pocket, ineptly hidden away, as if it weren't uniquely gifted at fooling people. But then my caution was forgivable, and forgiven, since it arose from love and from a beginner's ignorance about what the hand could do. And no one ever looked at me anyway; that was one of my more typical problems. When I walked down the sidewalk, I had to weave this way and that, and even step out of the stream of foot traffic into doorways or behind mailboxes, because people would have walked right into me if I hadn't, would have thrown me down and trampled me, stepped right on my face with their filthy soles and impaling high heels. But that time, the big man coming toward me on New Year's Day, heedless, eyes on his ridiculous phone—without a thought I waved at him, waved at him with my hand of glory, and he turned aside... or I should say, he was *turned* aside. Turned aside for me, who had always been the one to turn aside, not the one anybody would turn aside for. I passed him by, exultation in my throat, and I had to step into the doorway of an empty storefront to collect myself, to press my hand of glory to my chest and ask it to still my bursting heart.

I used to think that glory came to you after you did something, but now I understand that it comes first. Glory picks you out and strengthens you to do what must be done. Now I understand, the legend comes first. It is written. It is the beacon that pulls you out of the dark. The hand of glory unlocks all locks. It opens all doors and unravels all knots. It sheds a light that only I can see. It keeps the awoken awake and keeps the sleepers asleep. My first night with the hand on my arm, I went to bed so uncertain and afraid that I was shaking. I lay on my back, afraid to turn on my side, thinking I was going to vomit if I did. A painful sweat burst from every pore, it was like I was creaking with that antique electricity again. I didn't fall asleep, I didn't drift off uneasily in the old way. Instead, my soul pulled free of my body. It slept, but I stayed awake. The moment my soul got clear, the pain stopped; it was exactly like sliding into a pool on a hot day, except that the medium I joined didn't have the weight of water —it was lighter than air, a light I couldn't see, not yet, but that I felt sure I would learn to see. I felt my hand of glory taken by another hand that held it and drew me along. I felt the burning itch there where it joined my wrist, and I feared that something was trying to pull it off, and I would rather have died than let that happen—I wanted to double around my hand of glory like a cat coiling around a mouse, but the tension in my arm was not fierce, not predatory at all. The fear left me.

I was being led by the hand. I felt the fingers of my hand of glory close on that other hand, fibrous and inert, like papier-mâché. I couldn't see who was leading me, but I knew they weren't invisible, they weren't in the dark, they were lit up with light I couldn't see yet. They were going to lead me by my hand of glory to the light that it cast, and I would see them by that light then. I just wasn't different enough yet. But I had to try, that was part of it. Now that I think back on that night, I think I did see something, a flash of an outline, a stiff form maybe, just dimly illuminated against the unseeing—I can't call it darkness because it's full of light—it's the sleeping world that wants me to believe in it that puts the darkness between us. I have to keep pushing further into it to get through, to see the glory of awakening. In time, I will see the one leading me by my hand of glory.

...In the stories, the hand of glory is caricatured as a tool for thieves. What would burglars know about glory, the hidden light? Who could care about anything else, if they truly possessed glory already? If I'm going to be a thief, then I will be thief who steals back what is mine, all those stolen moments wasted trudging through one weary day after another, running errands for Mack, Mack and cousin Doris, Mack and Cousin Doris. Thin pretexts! I can hear laughter somewhere. I think it must be mine, too. They are going to throw me out of here. It won't be long before I hear their feet on the stairs. Let's go and see what he's been up to... I can't remember when I last went up there... All a dream, another bunch of blandishments conjured up by sleep to darken my path and keep me from glory, but I belong to glory now, or I know now that I always have... have always belonged to glory, always... I come and go, but the tinsel of life, the baubles and carols, are to be swept away. Now my task is to remember and meditate on what the hand shows me when my soul breaks free in the night, and nothing else. I'm done serving!

I know they are coming for me, and my hand of glory is ready.

The door to my room opens after a decorous knock. I never lock it any more—what do I need a lock for? Two of them, decked out in their badges and their city regalia, how cheaply bought! I show them what real glory looks like. I don't say a word, I just face them. I raise my hand of glory, and I light it.

That stopped them.

Since that night, my hand of glory has no further need for disguise but manifests itself for all to see in its true character. The sight is too much for them; they can't stand even the least reminder of their own blindness, although they would never admit it to themselves, let alone me—least of all me. Me, the one who knows them better than they know themselves! So, they compel me to keep it out of sight, wrapped in bandages, as if I were disfigured. They would see it that way. They speak to me deferentially, or with a false amiability tinged with fear, as is only right. They know what I said to them that night. Their agents, no doubt, were well-paid to relay it to them, word for word, as I knew they would. I spoke calmly, in a controlled voice, but the power of the hand was so great that my voice returned to me from the walls of my little room with such power they sounded like screams. I got a long look at them in the light that only I can see, hidden, not in a darkness that could only make it more conspicuous, but concealed in plain view, within the gold and orange of the fire. That's what the candle was always for, by the way, to hide the real light! To throw the shadows that confuse the sleepers and keep them sleeping while I watch them sleep, hovering over them. I study sleep and sleepers. I can see their souls bundled up in sleep. A dormitory—a spider's larder, victims drugged, bound, waiting. My hand aches in these wrappings. They're always too tight. They want to keep me bound up tight, like these others. Perhaps they hoped that one of them might take the hand from me. My hand, though... do they understand that my hand was never cut off from anyone but me? This is my hand! I took my birthright back when I pressed it to my wrist. How else can they account for the easy way I got rid of the false one—that's a point that's never even been raised. No one ever found it, did they? This hand chose me, came to me, was always mine, and so it can never be taken away, even if they cut it off. Is it any less mine if it's cut off?

The bandages may defend their eyes from the glory of my hand, but they can do nothing to balk its power. I still turn people from my path when I raise it, no door is locked to me—but what do I care about doors? No person is ever really closed to me, either; the light that only

I can see cannot fail to reveal who is awake and who is asleep, and I am always shocked anew when I realize just how many sleepers there are, and how many of those who pretend to the great wisdom are not only themselves sleepers, but among the most deeply asleep. Sleep, all who sleep. Awake, all who wake. My hand of glory will never let you learn the truth. It shines only for me. Perhaps that was a mistake I made. Too generous. That light is beautiful, the most beautiful thing of all. I haven't really seen it yet myself, but it's so beautiful I already know it in my heart.

There... at the end of the hall, around the corner, past the last office... the emergency door, ajar, as I must have wished! The hand cannot fail.

The chill and blaze of the new year, of January afternoon, falls on me like night. The daylight hides me. You know you don't belong there. You don't belong around people. That's always been true, hasn't it? We must cleave to those things that have always been true. My hand is pointing, through the bandages, to the horizon—west, I think. Even distance is no barrier to it any more. I can reach out—just let me unwrap it—reach out over the horizon and take hold of space, seize it in the grip of my long, new fingers and pull the distance toward me, pull it right up over the horizon like a heavy comforter, a distance that will stay distant from me even when I'm there, out where I will preside over a solitude so empty even I'm not there, forever alone in the awakened darkness of secret light with my hand of glory.

The Starving of Saqqara

I FIRST SAW them set off very dramatically in a case set alone in the middle of the gallery floor, lit from above and below, so that the light scoured every trace of shadow from the creased surfaces of the statue. I know I glanced at them as I came in, and then began drifting along the left-hand wall, allowing the framed images there to pass me by. But I wasn't looking at the images; I was too aware of the presence of those two behind me, waiting for the moment when I would turn to look at them. When I did, I couldn't leave them.

When the docents announced that the museum was closing, I abruptly turned and hurried away without a backward glance, feeling less embarrassment than shame, as if I'd been caught staring at something I shouldn't have been staring at. My feet ached, my back was stiff; I had been walking around and around the case for hours, it seemed. It was as if seeing them had set off slow music in me, which was gathering force. I went home and looked up images of them. I found a short film consisting of lingering close-ups edited together, fading in and out of each other, set to Debussy's "Clair de Lune."

What a perverse choice of music! Delicate, infused with a sense of discovery, it was meant to invoke images of familiar things all aglow in moonlight, under your gaze as you rest in a state of tranquil contemplation. You gaze in delight on a transformed world, enjoying an immortal calm that never entirely overcomes the memory of mortal transience. But what are you being shown? Two starving human beings, emaciated, squatting naked on the ground, half-buried in clay. There are still some traces of pigment left on them, mainly streaks of green on one of the faces... The bodies were carved from limestone, and in their extreme whiteness they still seemed to be exposed to the glare of a pitiless Egyptian sun. Two bound captives, with ropes around their necks. The back of one figure was gouged with unintelligible writing that no one had ever been able to identify. Their eyes still squinted; their mouths hung open as if they were panting for breath or crying out in misery. Was "Clair de Lune" selected because, as the camera inched over the surfaces of the huge, elongated heads of these figures, someone had been struck by a resemblance between their powdery, curved whiteness, and the surface of the moon?

I read that they were only two feet tall. To me, they had seemed life-sized. One was supposed to be male, the other female, but I couldn't distinguish that between them. Two ashen figures half-melted into a clay base—hairless, almost foetal figures with sticklike arms and legs, bulbous heads, noses broken away, knees pulled up to their chins, elbows flush to wizened torsos. They sit face to face, a little entangled in each other. One of them keeps its right fist lightly clutched to its breast, while the left hand holds the other by the arm, as though the one figure were trying to comfort the other. So, the statue was showing me a human being reduced to little more than a skeleton, a dying human being, who nevertheless was able to find in themselves a fleeting surplus, just enough to offer consolation to another dying human being.

I learned that the statue had appeared in Canada around 1950, in a collection belonging to some dealers in antique artifacts. No one could account for the name, which associated it with the necropolis of Memphis. The statue, I read, was either a unique example of pre-Dynastic Egyptian art, or a modern fake. I know nothing about Egyptian art, but the style struck me as modern. It wasn't just the stark contrast between "The Starving of Saqqara," with its anatomical irregularities, its curious posing, its unhieratic realism, and, on the other hand, the untroubled, suavely-poised and hieratic sculptures I'd seen in the Egyptian wing of the museum. It was the subject matter, above all, that seemed wrong. There were plenty of images of dominated peoples, captives and slaves, but they were always triumphalist caricatures. These figures, as distorted as they were, had too much real humanity, their suffering was too palpable; this was the kind of art 20th century people make, wasn't it?

Unless this *was* triumphalistic. I refused to believe it. Weren't the cruel caricatures of defeated Nubians a kind of denial, meant to defend the Egyptians against charges of a far worse cruelty? Portraying the conquered enemy as a sort of cartoon creature was a way to avoid acknowledging the horrors that had been and were yet still to be meted out in the course of that conquest, or at least that's what I had assumed. Only a monster would preserve this image of utter abjection in order to gloat over it.

Time and again I returned to the images of the statue. The eyes seem to squint in the sun. The bunched lids are crepey around bleary irises. The skin taut across the cheekbones, the teeth exposed, the withered lips drawn down in a fixed grimace, a harelip-like snarl, the mouth agape almost like a trumpet, strong chin unlike the receding chin of the other, both with overhanging brows and gauntly tall cheekbones. It's as if one of them were speaking, with that open mouth, the fragment of tongue remaining to it—speaking very matter-of-factly. Perhaps babbling, driven insane. The traces left by the hollows of the nostrils contribute to the impression that the noses were not broken away, but that the image depicts two people who have had their noses sliced off.

I found other images of starving people in Egyptian art, but in all of them the figures were bas-relief carvings of people with drawn but noble faces, mouths firmly set, cheeks sunken, symmetrical bands of protruding ribs, full heads of hair—or some covering for the head, with the usual linen wrapper around the hips, and reaching out, making all manner of angular gestures with their lean arms. Nowhere did I see any crouched, cringing figures like "The Starving of Saqqara." It was as if the sculpture had been formed to give the lie to those other, statelier, or at least more impersonal, images. But I couldn't find any way to release myself from the horrifying idea that someone had ordered this statue made as it was, to revel in it. Was this some kind of trophy? The problem with that idea was that these figures were not characteristic enough to be particular people, some hated enemy who had finally been served their due comeuppance, a traitor, a tyrant, a blasphemer. These were nobodies. The whole point, unavoidably, was that these people were just people, any people.

When I returned the next day, they weren't there. A terse note had been propped up in the display case. "This object is unavailable." When I asked the guard standing in the doorway with a look of philosophical boredom on her face, all she could tell me was —

"They didn't bring it out today."

So, they took it "in" somewhere, after closing time?

Eventually I found a docent who told me that something had gone wrong with the lights that illuminated that particular display case, and the statue had been removed until the lights could be repaired. She had no idea how long that would take. I considered asking if I could see the statue wherever it now was, but the circumstances were so confusing, and I had so many other things on my mind, that I didn't manage it. Were they boxed up somewhere, or just sitting out on a table, perhaps just on the other side of that wall? Perhaps I could see them through a window, if they were in the basement, beneath this floor. But would they be stored away as they were, uncovered? Wouldn't they have to be covered, especially if they were in the basement, and the basement were as damp as basements usually are? Museum basements may have better climate control though. Could I claim to be some sort of student or academic, or arrange a private viewing? Perhaps I could pay to see it?

I found myself in the gift shop, staring at a photograph of them, on a postcard. The two figures together, in icy blackness, and from far enough away that their anguish was not really discernible. The impulse to buy it nearly gave way to another impulse, which was to pull the sheaf of cards from display rack and rip them to shreds. No one should look at this! Or, not like this, not on a postcard—it was like playing "Clair de Lune," using this image of horrible suffering as the backdrop to "wish you were here, grandma is fine, blah blah blah."

The exhibit had been nearing the end of its run. Why had I waited so long to see it? Soon, they would be returning everything to a storeroom at Concordia University. I returned every day, until I had gotten to know half the staff it seemed, but the promised restoration never happened. The statue was never brought back out again. The exhibit closed, but I couldn't just leave them there, all alone in some storage area. I had the stupid impulse to loiter around the museum as long as I knew that they were somewhere inside, but of course they could just as readily be stored somewhere else, couldn't they? How could I find out where? I spent much of my scant free time searching for images of them, for writings about them, more to keep in contact with them than out of any desire for knowledge. Knowing things about them was not unimportant to me, but it was only a means to an end. I couldn't leave them.

If it weren't for this persistent searching, I would almost certainly have overlooked the news that they had gone missing. No one was prepared to call it a theft, not yet, although that possibility had of course not been ruled out, either, not by any means. After the defect in their display lighting had been found, the two of them had been shifted to "storage"—whatever that means—and then it appears they were never quite accounted for after that. Someone at the museum, a person with whom, as it happens, I had spoken more than once, was quoted, saying that there might have been a miscommunication about the statues requiring restoration or cleaning. It seems that the antiquities at the museum were not kept under constant watch, but were simply set aside, now here, now there, not at random, of course, not by any means, but without the constant supervision that would have, more or less, been their best protection against theft. How could anyone leave them unprotected? How could anyone leave them, at all?

It seemed to me that all this meant they were still here, somewhere in town. Perhaps not. They might have been taken away, but I would have felt that, I think. It just didn't seem plausible, though, that they, while, if not full-sized, are certainly not small, and not especially robust either, I think, could be spirited out of town with any dispatch. I mean, it could be done, of course, but not quickly or discreetly. And where would you send them? Wouldn't it make more sense to keep them here in town, out of sight, for a while?

— Did I take them?

I don't remember taking them.

I live alone. It's true I could have taken them, if I had known where they were.

But, of course, I didn't know where they were. Where are they now? Did I take them and forget I'd done it?

It's possible, but then knowing what is and isn't possible is just a guessing game, and besides, what good does it do me to concern myself with that now? If I took them, then I would know where they are, and I don't, do I?

They aren't at home—a painstaking search proved that. I don't know if I've taken them, but I... *feel*... as though I have. This feeling is intolerable. It's an intolerable feeling! I can't think or sleep or eat. I jump at every sound, can't speak to anyone for fear I'll blurt out an incoherent admission or worse, a stream of false language. It is necessary—absolutely necessary—to do something. They're out there alone, somewhere, in someone's hands—I imagine them being treated roughly, an arm breaking, and I can hear my own sharply indrawn breath, my shoulders rise, my throat stopping. I have to find them.

I was lying flat on my back, dreaming, of course, unable to move in the bed, and they were in the apartment with me, somewhere very near me, and I heard scraping on the floor, steadily nearer. The sheet beneath me was yanked and yanked again, not hard. I saw the tops of their heads. My head was flat on the mattress, fixed upright, but out of the corner of my left eye, I could see the tops of their heads. The bed dipped with their weight. Stiff, dry lips touched my exposed left calf, little hands gripped my leg feebly, and then teeth sank into the muscle. I screamed in agony. The jaws closed, tugged, tearing the muscle, the pain grew worse and became a sick horror. A shadow came between me and the ceiling. A hard, cold face nuzzled my chin upwards. Teeth cut into my throat. I couldn't scream any more, I had woken up, alone, unharmed but unable to breathe.

They had been silent, apart from the rustling of the bedclothes as they moved. They were stiff, like wooden figures, and in the dream I had thought the jaws were made of wood and hinged like wooden jaws, and they hadn't been ravenous, or hungry, or anything, but had acted with a silent and dispassionate automation. They didn't know what they were doing, they were beyond knowing anything, and ate what could no longer nourish them in any way. Silent, numb, and mindless, they had torn into me as if it were all they *could* do. I spent the day looking for them. The dream had destroyed my appetite; I busied myself looking for them all day long, until I was staggering with hunger.

I checked the area in the vicinity of the museum first, not because I expected to find them there, although I couldn't rule out the possibility that the thieves, if there were any, had attempted to hide them in plain sight, not far from the museum, but more so because I roughly knew where they had been kept, and I wanted to plot out the most likely route they might have taken out of the building. I determined that the thieves, if there were any, would have almost certainly parked their van, or whatever vehicle they were using, on the street at a point nearest the best exit—which was not the closest one to the storage area, not by any means, since that exit was pretty exposed to public view at nearly all times, and which for that matter had a tall flight of stairs to manage as well. The best exit was one of two service exits at ground level. Both of these were about equidistant from the storage rooms, but one of them opened on a loading area that was overlooked by tall buildings on two sides, lit well at night, and visible from the street; the other exit, however, was tucked away behind a low wall that concealed some of the dumpsters, and which would screen anyone emerging from that exit until they'd traversed about half the distance from the building to the sidewalk. There was no fence there, either. If, for example, a van had been parked adjacent to that exit, someone, that is, a pair of reasonably strong persons, could readily carry even a large object from the exit to the van and load it up in less than a minute. And it was a one-way street, so it was possible to trace their likely route as far as the corner. From there, the choice was obvious. A right turn was impossible—that street was one way too—a left turn would involve circling the museum and entering a neighborhood with virtually no through traffic, since it was a sort of promontory thrust out into the bay. The van must have gone straight ahead. That meant they were heading for the highway. If that were their route, then the thieves, if there were any, were long gone, and could be anywhere.

But, wouldn't they have been safer here in town? Was it wise to transport them a long distance, rattling around in the back of a van? The museum couldn't have packed them for transport already; under those circumstances, that is, if they had packed them, then surely they would know their whereabouts. There couldn't be more than one loading area in the museum. So, the two of them must have been sitting out, under a simple throw cover at best. The thief or thieves didn't have time to pack them carefully before they removed them from the building. It was impossible to secure them in the car. The thief, if he wanted to preserve them from harm, stopped somewhere nearby, after as short a trip as was consistent with avoiding discovery, in order to secure them for a longer trip. For that, it would be necessary to find a place near the museum with a loading bay, or at least a decent-sized entrance, off the street; and it would have to be empty. There was no sense in risking discovery, signing leases and so on. The thing to do was to drive them to an empty building with a loading bay off the street. There had to be a bay, because securing them meant crating them, and a bulky crate is not going to fit through an ordinary door.

I drove around all day until my head swam, and I realized I was bound for an accident. I kept going and going, circling blocks, feeling sure that, the moment I saw the right building, I would know, but the sidewalks were busy with people, there were lights in all the windows, commerce everywhere, and it was no place for them. Where were they? By the end of the day I had to pull over. My hands were shaking. What was happening, what was *being done* to them? They existed, they were lost, in motion somewhere in the world around me, and in danger, terrible danger.

They returned to me again in a dream that night. When I awoke, it seemed as though I'd been dreaming that dream throughout the night, nine hours of it. They were there, by the window, and the glare of the day fell on them like the heat of the noonday sun, so that it seemed to consume them without reducing them, as if something is cruelly replenishing that incessant loss. I can feel them shrinking from the light, but they are statues, and they cannot move. I'm afraid to move them myself. I imagine breaking one of their arms in a clumsy attempt to drag the statue out of the light, and the figure wailing in helpless agony. After what might have been hours, it occurs to me at last to cover the window, since, now that I think about it, the sun has not budged in the sky all this time. I waste time in a fruitless search for a curtain, a sheet, a piece of cardboard, and in the silence, I can imagine their weak voices raised in pain. I feel it in my own throat. I feel the light like acid on my skin. I turn my head, and I am face to face with one of them, staring directly into eyes that seem about to vanish in sheer suffering, my own lips just inches from the gaping, stinking mouth, and I realize that I can't see the other one because I *am* the other one, and I cannot move, cannot move, not even to pull myself aside into the shade and out of the searing light of the pitilessly motionless sun.

I returned to the area I had scouted the previous day and continued searching; a region bounded on one side by the street I had first taken, and on the other by an enormous public park. There were plenty of hiding places in there, I was sure, but, as there were no roads leading into the park, but only surrounding it, anyone with a large object to conceal would have had to carry it in plain sight over broad lawns, or past fountained plazas and circles that are never entirely empty of people. Not possible, of course. Toward the end of a nerve-wracking day of wasted effort, I suddenly remembered—with a palpable shock that, for a moment, I feared might be the beginning of some sort of seizure—that the domain of converted industrial buildings and warehouses I had been searching did not quite end when it reached the park: there was a little more on the far side, between the park and the river.

I knew it was the place when the first dingy brick buildings came into view through the trees. There were far fewer people on the street, fewer shop fronts. The streets were in good repair, but empty even of parked cars, and while the buildings weren't dilapidated, they were clearly abandoned. It was as if the place were waiting for the spirit of some new city to wipe it away. I parked my car in the middle of the first block I came to, the only car at the curb on either side of the street. I needed to proceed slowly. I would have to peer in through windows and stare for many minutes at a time into the dark crevasses separating the buildings. I would be waiting, too.

It was already late in the day. When the sun set, the night poured into the street, flooded the buildings, and engulfed me. The streetlights did not come on. No matter where I stood, I could not see the lights of the city anywhere, and, as the stars came out—the same stars that had shone down on them when they were born, when they trembled in the sudden chill of the desert at night—the solitude of the place began to frighten me. The absence of people began to seem like a disguise, hiding the presence of many. I stopped and listened. I couldn't hear the city roar. This was a piece of the city, empty of anyone but me, or so it seemed, come loose in time and drifting in space. I knew they were there, in a pocket of horror tucked away somewhere in one of these dead buildings, behind the portentously uncracked and transparent glass of these windows and screened from view by weather-beaten, strictly regular rows of brick and mortar. It wasn't until I'd slammed myself into my car—with a loud crash that seemed to die away into the muffling air outside—that I realized I'd been unable to stand the exposure of that street at night. It was as if the city were watching me with bated breath, withholding its light, to see what I would do, to see me find them. I couldn't stand it. I had to return home again. Things had changed. It was clear, by the time I'd let myself back in, that things had changed. It was because I had been right. They were still here, in town, and they were there, in that little cluster of empty blocks on the far side of the park. Tomorrow I would go there, and I would find them.

That night, I was at the outskirts of the city, consulting with various of my colleagues about some matters of importance involving water, irrigation. Our formal conversation at an end, one of my colleagues starts to press me about something; we are both avidly interested, even obsessed, with art of all kinds, and especially pictorial and sculptural arts. We are men of high rank in the city, so we are sure to be invited when a new statue is presented or when a carved wall or pillar is unveiled, and in our own modest ways we both collect what we can. Now he has something remarkable to show me, he says, and conducts me to the home of a mutual acquaintance, one of the wealthiest and most powerful officials in all Memphis, and a noted patron of the arts. As we meet with him, exchanging ceremonious words and gestures, I am becoming short of breath, all the blood pooling in my center, leaving my arms and legs weak and cold, and my heart bristles and shakes, because this man is gesturing to the tomblike door of his home, and I know what's inside, what he is going to show me. It's them. Freshly made, fully intact and new, and there is no doubt that I am going to read the words scrawled on them, to be able now to read them and understand what they mean. I'm being waved through the door. My friend has my arm, I can't stop walking forward. Any moment I am going to see them *in their entirety*—

I wake up with a strangled cry, shivering as waves of cold revulsion and misery wash over me, nearly crazy with the desire to rip the life out of myself and get out of the world.

If I find them, the dreams won't stop, will they? Will they become permanent?

The block was just as empty by day as by night, and nearly as silent. I found I could move in and out of the buildings easily. Most of them had no doors to lock, nothing was boarded up or marked, and being there was like visiting the world after it had ended.

I had scaled one building and then a second. I was looking out into a shaft way from the rear windows when I saw the crowns of two misshapen white heads just above the sill of a window opposite.

I fly down the stairs, out into the street, which wheels and skates along with me, carrying me to the doorway, propelling me up the stairs and through an open doorway into a vast apartment, the entire floor open, the partitions torn away, all plaster and drywall—and them, by the window.

"I found you!" I say, rushing toward them, hating the sight of them but needing to take hold of them, as if I were going to gather them up like lost children, and indeed my arms are nearly entirely around them when they turn their horror-stricken, imploring eyes to me, and recoil from my touch, shrinking, crying out in pain, in fear, and raise their impotent, shaking hands to beseech me not to hurt them again.

The Purlieus

THE MAN SWAYED, looking at me, but somehow incompletely.

"Mind if I sit?" he asked. "I won't say anything."

I had the impulse to quit the bench and leave it to him. The day was passing, the lights would be coming on soon. I liked to sit here and watch them come on sometimes; it was a way of restoring myself a bit before the long train ride home. The man smelled like liquor, and his head drooped beneath a grey veil of heavy drunkenness I could almost see. He reminded me of someone I knew once, though, and the pang of memory kept me from getting up.

"Go ahead," I told him.

He sat heavily, his hands between his thighs, slumped back against the seat. He threw his head back then and let it sag back, lifting his chin and shutting his eyes, which I now saw were bright with tears. I took him for a professional run up against some tragedy. He sighed, and sighed again, rubbed his face, and went slack, sighing.

"Are you all right?" I asked.

"Yeah," he said, rubbing his face again, and seeming to draw his head from his shoulders with effort. I saw alarm flash in his eyes. "Am I disturbing you?" he asked me. "I'm sorry."

He said this with such a woeful expression that I couldn't help taking an interest in him.

"Things were so much simpler when we were kids," he said.

I felt my interest start to evaporate.

"You know there wasn't... all this..."

He waved his hand to designate "all this," meaning perhaps the city, the traffic, the park, the passing of time, the crowds streaming on the distant sidewalks, the indifference of all this man-made business.

"Or, well, there was, but... none of it meant anything, you didn't know what the hell it all meant, but you believed what they told you about it..."

I excused myself and began to get up.

"I remember..." he said, his voice becoming wistful, "... I read this book when I was a boy... I wish I could remember the name... Maybe you read it, too... It was set in England, around Edwardian times, on a country estate or something, something in the country, and it was about a boy who met this girl. Her name was... Snowy, I think... You okay?"

I did not return his look. I kept my eyes fixed straight ahead.

"Just a cramp. I get them sometimes."

"...Mm," he said, letting his head drop. The sound of traffic replaced his voice for a while.

"Snowy... Snowy Amworth, that was her name."

"...Anyway... " he said at last, "the boy and the girl find, like, an enchanted spot, a magical spot, in the... the fields."

He says the word "fields" with a fleeting delight in his voice, and, for an instant, a sort of golden light seems to play over the dull greenish-black slope before me.

"...and there's something they do there, they meet with the beast that lives there... and it's wonderful... and the little girl... she's not wanted at home... and she keeps going back to the spot because, it's like there's no place else for her..."

The man sighs again. I can sense the sorrow welling up from deep within him, filling his voice, and throwing a shadow over him. I turn to look at him again. His face weaves back and forth before me, very faint in the lights of the buildings far away, shining through the trees.

"...and there's an offer... made... and she takes it... she commits suicide... the boy finds out too late, and he comes... and he sees her... sees her go..."

And now fear lifts up out of him, blending itself with the sorrow—

"...and he sees something come... the demon... it comes to receive... receive Snowy... and then it looks just like her, and she, her body, doesn't look like her anymore, the way a dead body doesn't look like the person it was... the demon walks away with her, her appearance."

The man sobs, twice. "Sorry. It was so sad."

My left hand flashes through the air and closes on his throat. The man stares at me, eyes wide, saying things, inchoate things, like "hey" and "what" and "leave me —"

"How did you find me?"

I climb on top of him, pinning him, clutching his neck. I shake him.

"Who sent you?"

The man jabbers, fumbling at me.

"You're talking to *me? About Snowy?*" I ask him through gritted teeth, giving him another shake. I'm trembling, I'm seeing white. The man bucks beneath me, finally getting the idea, beginning, too late, to struggle in my grasp, but I have him pinned, my weight is on him.

"Did it send you? Did it send you? *Did it?*"

The lights of the park come on, backlighting the huge boulder behind the bench, blinding me with its sudden glare. I push down onto him, and he buckles under me.

"*Where is she?*"

My voice is low, but it tears my throat. The man stops struggling.

I glanced back as I ran down the hill, and before I had enough sense to slow to a quick walk, a less suspicious walk, I caught a glimpse of his hand protruding from the shadow that engulfed the bench, palm up, like someone begging for money. The hand was disembodied, amputated by the hard edge of the shadow that concealed the rest of him. My own hands ached; he'd pummeled and battered me, but my grip had only tightened and tightened. Tightened until his body had finally gone slack, more and more slack. Questions raced through my mind, repeating—who sent him, what sent him, why now? *Where is she?*

I can't say how long it's been since I've slept; it must be at least two days. All the same, I seem to be sleeping all the time. Leaves drip water on to me. How did the water get on the leaves? Why does it fall only on me? Out of every shadow of a certain darkness his hand is extended toward me, palm up, like someone begging, but even without such shadows, even without... there's the sound I felt in my palms and fingers, the humming tube his neck was in my hands, filled with pent up breath I wouldn't let out. A choked gurgling is embedded in my hands like my own pulse, perhaps forever. I dunk both my hands in a sink of cold water and hold them there for as long as I can stand it, until my bones light up with cold, but that little tickle his Adam's apple left against my palms is still there.

I don't want to forget; I can't afford to, because I have to avoid being caught. The body still hasn't been found—or if it has, they're keeping the news to themselves. And why wouldn't they? I can't imagine a body lying there on park bench, unnoticed, for at least two days. Since there's no word about the body anywhere, I have to assume the police found it first, and got it out of there early in the morning, even before the sunrise, the early morning police, so there was nothing for anyone to see except, maybe, a sheeted figure on a stretcher. Where was the worried family? The announcement that someone had gone missing, the urgent request for information? If he were all alone in the world, why wouldn't he have done his drinking at home? Why come to the park, if not to sober up for someone else's sake? Why unburden yourself to a stranger, if not to conceal something from your family?

But he wasn't a stranger, because what stranger would have known about Snowy? This is precisely where the story finally begins to make sense: daunted at the last minute by the task he had been sent to perform, the man had bolstered his courage, or really his effrontery, his insolence, his duplicity, with a few drinks first. He must have thought that a show of drunkenness would have made it easier for him to approach me and draw me into an ostensibly spontaneous conversation, but he overdid it, became actually drunk. The rendezvous had been fixed; whoever sent him knew I was entering the park, on my way to the bench I'd picked out as my own, and that it might be a long time, weeks, before I came back again to that spot, which had to be that very spot and that only, that only... the spot where he would sound me out, a selected, a carefully selected and isolated spot where he would sound me out, find out just what I know, or no, they knew that already—the point, as I have already determined, to take Snowy away from me.

The thought of Snowy washes over me. All my love for her, incessantly reviving, overwhelming me again. A scrap of lace lying bright in a shop window, the ideal perfume of blooming wisteria, the intimate cry of the mourning dove, and all my love for her revives. This is what had to be prevented, but the game was dangerous; it backfired, and fully resurrected the love that I was born to give to her. I'd never forgotten her, no matter what anyone might have thought, any more than I could ever have forgotten the terror of what was done to her, that I alone saw, no matter what anyone else says. They've even written a book about it, to discredit me, and even then, they couldn't help making it beautiful or showing me in my true light.

I see her rushing to embrace her dying mother on her deathbed. Luminous in the shadowy sickroom, her face mingled anguish and beauty to stop the heart, and to dominate my memory like a religious emblem. Where was I? In my mind's eye, it's almost as if I had been standing like a ghost submerged in the wall by the bed, but then I must have been looking in through a window—and, now that I think of it, I do recall the window frame and the white of the wall outside, crawling with moonlit columns of ants. I was a boy her age then. Perhaps I stood on a rock or a low wall. That might account for my elevated point of view.

Fire blooms in my chest whenever I recall the gently abashed way she told me her name was Snowy, Snowy Amworth, knowing it was a peculiar name, knowing that it was also a charming name, although she could not have known how strong that charm would be, that she was casting a lifelong spell on me. She claimed every flake of snow I would ever see, and, at the same time, the soft and fragrant air of summer twilight into which she always seemed about to dissolve, and with which she always seemed about to become one, Snowy, name of my life.

Bisected by a shadow, a truncated arm... the open palm hangs open in front of me. You wanted me to put her name into that palm? You got what you deserved. I know exactly what's going on, and I'm not naive about the role the police are playing in it, hiding your death, even making believe you're still alive, all because it wasn't enough, what you did to her—and that's the only thing that makes sense, that you are part of it too. You were all against Snowy, and us, everything was, everything but nature, which you hate, the trees and the sky, which you mock, the quiet at the Purlieus, the sound of the fountain and the birds in the drowsy haze, which you sneer at—so you want her memory now? It wasn't enough, the image you took from her, you have to filch her image from my memory too, because I loved her, and so some of her life still lives in me? And you've come after me at last. You've finally worked up the nerve to come after me and try to take it from me, after all these years. But who did you send? A drunk?

Was that really the attempt on my memory? Or was it a trap—to provoke me to murder, and to give yourselves a pretext to make away with me? Arrest me, drag me to prison, extract her memory from my mind at your leisure then? But then, why waste a man's life like that, when you could have pulled me right off that bench? Something is apparently restraining you. You're the types who can't move in straight lines. You wanted me to disclose something, didn't you? Let me drift into her memory, and that would expose her to you, your seizure. Then you could finish the job, is that it? With me as an accomplice, and that accusation you knew would destroy me?

Well, that didn't work out so well for you, did it? How are you going to catch me unawares now? What a blunder!

When at last I do sleep, I see the man's eyes in the shadow. I am up above him, kneeling on him, my head in the light and his below, in a shadow that closes over his face like the surface of a lake. I hold him under. The swimming eyes are barely visible, only two crescent gleams in the nebulous pallor of the contorted face, full of unfeigned shock and fear. And now, with hatred too? They appear below me, not quite from beneath the floor, screened by a sheet of light from the lamp that falls between us like a lid on the shadow. What are you doing here? That's what they're asking.

Despite myself my mind returns to what I saw in late September, when I screamed Snowy's name so hard I felt my soul leave my body— when Snowy fell among the trees and her neck snapped—when I saw the beast slithering toward her from the shuddering curtains of leaves and the shadows beneath the blue stones, like a coruscating amalgam of every part of the day, and leaned over her, you, Snowy, and when it stood up straight, it turned its face, now your face, to see me and to try its new smile on me, its nightmarish smile. That day I stood over you. I looked down on you. I saw your face wasn't yours any more. "The wind rose in the trees, stirring the mourning doves." You didn't look like yourself, because that thing from the woods, the beast, took your likeness—and still has it, after all these empty years. Hiding behind those empty years now, turning them into the haunted, sacred forest by the Purlieus. The smile even now tries to destroy your real image, it gnashes its teeth in my memory, a bullet hole in the portrait, it gibbers, bites, shatters the sunlit day like painted glass. But nothing can stop you from floating back up into view as you were when you hurried to your mother's bedside, framed in the window I looked through. Nothing could have prevented you from looking at the little painting hidden inside the wall, even knowing what that would mean for someone in your family. Nothing can prevent your name and image from being the banner planted in me that makes me who I am, and that I am still who I am is my triumph over the beast. You gave your life, your smile, your face, because you loved me. You sacrificed yourself for me, Snowy.

There's still nothing anywhere about the murder, the body. The palpable sensation of his throat in my hands hasn't faded. I know that I killed a real man, and not a sending. I can't sleep, though, and that's a problem. It's beating me down. A confession to the police might enable me to sleep, but more likely it would mean placing myself under the sway of the beast.

Nothing in my daily routine is disturbed. No one is the wiser. Some say I look a little tired, a bit under the weather, and suggest I take a sick day or two, but everyone is so bound up in their own problems that they haven't got much attention to spare for me. Otherwise, my days follow on with comforting regularity; being too tired to think is in some ways a help to me in my work, and even though that outstretched hand begging alms is always floating somewhere in my field of vision, I don't suppose anyone else can see it. No one has asked me about it.

But now, down the long hallway, raked with the golden light of late September that the window louvers break apart, golden light that shouldn't be there, a figure I know vanishing just now at the end, stepping just out of sight, a grown woman, a white skirt—I hear the word whispered—

"Snowy!"

My voice screaming it in my memory, in silence. I'm frozen in place for only a moment. My head light and my hands and feet like ice, I rush after you, not a little girl but a full-grown woman, as if she had never fallen—

Now I can't stop panting, and in my sleepless condition I feel like I'm going to faint, and I hurry to the bathroom to splash water on my face. No towels. I rub my face with my hands and dry them beneath the blower, lean against the wall my face dripping onto the floor, swaying.

The beast is here. It's the day of the Purlieus isn't it? Why the hell didn't I remember? Haven't I always taken special care of this day?

It can't come for me directly. These things can only come at us in golden light at sunset, in the shadow of the old beech trees and the gnarled roots of oak trees. The beast can bring these things along, and make them, but it can only get me if I come to it, if I allow myself to be tricked or confused by what I see around me instead of sticking closely to my own inner guidance. Step one, get out of the bathroom; step two, get out in public where you can be seen, where there are witnesses.

The corridor is empty, but footsteps are coming, almost padding. Run downstairs then—what a risk I'm taking! Or is it the police? Will I rush outside and find them there, smiling?

Coming up the stairs toward me, with a sheaf of papers in her arms.

"Snowy!"

Your face, so like hers and just a little like her face at her mother's bedside in the little tremor of alarm—the one I saw die—and go away smiling, belonging to something else—the name that echoes now up the stairwell. She's lunging back with a feigned start of surprise, and the flash of a golden band on one of the fingers that darts its gleams into my eyes, making them blink, and my body twists and footing wavers on the top step. Golden light! September!

My feet push me back from the brink and away from that thing with your likeness, aged and unlike my memory—*unlike* my memory. It's changed you, not just maturing. Not Snowy Amworth anymore. That is, I remember you because you don't look like you did – that's the trick. If you looked the same, I couldn't remember you because I would be seeing you, not remembering you, and I have to remember you, because they want that memory torn out of me like a beating heart to eat. Coming toward me up the stairs with a sheaf of papers and her face over nothingness, the beast, over the memory of a day and a fall and the faint noise of bone breaking in the spine.

I ran back into the corridor, I did not take the bait, the golden light warned me. I hurried to the other side of the building and ran down the stairs two at a time thinking it would be there and finding nothing, the open door, the street burning with the dazzling light of the sun.

Was it today? Or tomorrow? Was this only a warning, or was I too alert? Or am I counting on everything to be over? I look back at the building, to see if your face is there in any of the windows—nothing there. They're trying to panic me, to see what I will do. My feet take me uncertainly toward the park...

But why would I go there, if not to incriminate myself? Or am I going to find his corpse lying sprawled on a bench behind a huge boulder, one hand outstretched palm up?

I'm not a murderer. I don't want anything but to breathe air like the air of that day, filled with the smells of a late summer forest baked by the sun, and remember what was, not what was taken. The beast wants me to believe that it, something like the beast, must be a part of any day like that. It might not be lying. But the risk is the risk of love, the love that engulfed me whenever I saw you, Snowy, and that made my life ring in me like a bell, and that nothing has ever been able to revive, not even dreams. Was that you, Snowy, on the stairs? Or am I meant to torment myself with that question? There was no murder, Snowy, and there was no encounter on the stairs. All this is the beast's fantasy. I am still myself, the young boy who has always loved you and always will, and we are still running together in the light and shade of the beeches and oaks by the Purlieus. Don't go back into the park. Those aren't real trees. It isn't a real park. Be normal, do normal things, don't let on, don't show variation.

I go back to my apartment without hurrying. The sun is just below the horizon as I turn the keys in the door; its light remains in the sky even though it has vanished from sight. I step inside and set my keys down on the table by the door, same as always. I don't turn the lights on; while I am usually home earlier, I do not give myself permission to deviate from my normal routine. Leave the lights off for now, and search. No one must be here. If I turn the lights on, that would be the signal for it to appear, if it is here, waiting for me already. Could I out-run the beast? But that's what I've been doing all this time!

I am a little afraid to turn the lights on because the apartment doesn't really seem familiar, or I can't be sure if it is familiar or if it isn't. It's more impersonal than it should be. Uncharacteristic, like a hotel room; it has none of the special flavor that makes a place home for someone. It's my apartment, though – the same number, the same place in the building, the key fits the lock, the view out the glass balcony doors is the same, the furniture.

I cross the living room, toward the unpartitioned kitchen corner. Dimming light pours in through the sliding glass doors, as if there were some urgency to draining the light from the sky now that the sun was below the horizon. I never go out there. The light washes through the apartment in a golden glare that seems to darken and cloud the objects I see, as if it were smoke rather than light.

There is the short hallway, leading back to the bedroom; and there's the bathroom door, the bookcase, and on the shelf, directly in front of my eyes just now, faded golden letters on a narrow black spine.

I pull the book down. It's an old edition, dustjacket gone, frayed binding, pages smudged. I open to the first page.

The Purlieus
by Thomas Waveney
Grant Richards
London
1907

My own name is printed on the blank page opposite, in a child's handwriting.

The book has some scant illustrations, all black and white sketches, mingled in with the writing. I let it fall open. Snowy Amworth is framed on the white page all squirming with black writing, rushing to her mother's bedside—the book opens to it naturally, again and again. Even when I shut it, and try to put it back on the shelf, it seems to spring open to that page, obstinately returning to Snowy Amworth, who looked at the secret painting hidden in the wall, and whose neck snapped when she fell from a tree one golden afternoon, and whose likeness was stolen from her by the beast they had met together in the timeless glens behind a country house named *The Purlieus*. I close the book more firmly, pressing it shut with both hands, push it on to the shelf, but it slips from my fingers and drops to the floor. I don't see where it went.

I get down on my knees to search for it, still in the gathering darkness and silence.

I can't find it anywhere, not under the furniture, nowhere. On my hands and knees, I look up, around, to see if, in some way, it slid across the floor and ended up somewhere strange. I look toward the sliding glass balcony doors. The light coming in from the corridor outside mingles with the glow of appliance clocks in the stale air. With the darkening of the sky, the glass doors are beginning to reflect the room. In that reflection I see only the bare, anonymous furniture, the unlived-in kitchen and dinette area. The reflected bookcase is empty. The closet by the front door stands open, the post inside is a pale line in the dark, and there are no clothes hangers on it, no clothing, no boxes on the shelf above, no jumble of shoes on the floor. My jacket is gone from its hook by the door. My keys are not on the table. I fix my gaze on the spot where they should be, where I know I've just set them down, with the memory of the clink they made against the tabletop.

I know that my image must be there, in the center of the glass doors. My image, superimposed on the balcony, on all fours, my head thrust back against my shoulders, my face staring stupidly out over my splayed hands, searching for the book. The image must be there: a haggard, frightened man on hands and knees, down on the floor to look for an old childhood copy of *The Purlieus*—not a figure bent over, only to stand again when they have the likeness of the dead, the dead, but my gaze stays riveted to the spot on the table where my keys are not, because I am afraid, so afraid to know that what's reflected in that polished glass, after all, is an apartment for rent, untenanted, long empty, and where I should be, there will be only a space—the bare floor between the bookcase and the sofa.

Saccade

LISTEN TO ME: you are blind. You don't think you're blind. I am not speaking metaphorically; you, like most of mankind, are physically blind to certain visual stimuli. Yes, ultraviolet, infrared, these are colors we can't see, but then there is also saccadic blindness. Your eyes are not fixed in a mannikin-stare. They are constantly in motion, even—I would say, especially—when they are focused on one particular object. Stare at anything, no matter how steadily, how intently, and your eyes will still not quite freeze in place. To look attentively at an object, it is necessary for the eyes to make countless little adjustments. The name for an adjustment of the position of the eye is "saccade." That's how it always is, you eventually came to realize, here in the city's heart: you know nothing, and you're basically happy to, as if you think your own shell of semi-wilful ignorance protects you from having to worry about the bugs in the walls as opposed to the ones which occasionally crawl out of the drain, the man who might be slowly losing his mind behind that door across the way as opposed to the very obviously crazy guy who capers each morning on the corner of your street. Not to mention whether that cheerfully drunk lady in the unit to your right, who you see fumble with her keys every evening, will doze off one night with a lit cigarette in her hand and burn the whole fucking building down.

You're familiar with what they call "shaky-cam"? It refers to a type of cinematography. A hand-held camera is employed to give the audience a greater sense of immersion in the scene. The motion of the camera is intended to mimic the motion of the head and eye of a participant, or near witness. Watching a film shot in this manner can be disorienting, even nauseating. Perhaps you know what I mean? But, why should that be? Look around. Look at my hand. Look at the wall, those pipes—look at them!—the toolbox, the work bench.

Well, perhaps a custodian's closet isn't the best place for this experiment, at least not the best lighting, but you see what I mean? As you shifted your eye from one thing to another, from one side of your field of vision to another and then back, and as your eye focused itself on near things and then on more distant things, did you get queasy? Did any of that make you feel sick? Dizzy? Of course not. And yet, if you were to reproduce the same sequence of eye and head motions that you just performed using a *camera*, the scene as filmed would be instantly recognizable as a "shaky-cam" styled scene, and the viewer might well complain of disorientation or nausea if the sequence were extended long enough. Would you become nauseous if I continued to ask you to look now at this, now at that?

What's the difference, then? Why should "shaky-cam" footage be sickening to a viewer whose own vision is constantly shifting its perspective, darting from object to object? The difference is that human beings, and indeed most animals—are you listening? this is important! I'm telling you about something that your brain is doing without your being aware of it. This is scientifically-proven fact! Your brain is editing the visual information fed into it by your optic nerve, and the effect of this editing is something technically known as "saccadic blindness." That's not "psychotic" but "saccadic" – spelled s a c c a d i c.

Basically, your brain suppresses information that comes along the optic nerve whenever the eye makes a saccade. The camera and the optic nerve both register everything that happens within their field of sensitivity, so, when you watch the "shaky-cam" footage, you will see the image streaking when the camera moves. Your own vision also streaks whenever your eye makes a saccade, but your brain interrupts the signal to prevent the streak from registering. This is why you are able to look around, to focus now on this object, now on that, without becoming queasy or disoriented. Try it. Look around. You should notice a blip in your vision whenever you transfer your attention from one thing to another; the blip is more pronounced as the movement of the eye becomes greater. Go ahead, look at my hand, and now look over there, at the faucet. You see? You probably noticed a bit of a streak, but did you see how it cut off almost the moment it started? The way the streak didn't carry all the way over from my hand to the faucet? Your vision started to streak, but then suddenly you were looking at the sink, I mean the faucet, and you can't recall or visualize clearly what your eye saw on the way from the one object to the other. That's saccadic blindness. Your brain is actively suppressing what your eye sees when it moves. If it didn't, you would be as afflicted by simply looking around your environment as you are watching a "shaky-cam" film; "shaky-cam" would be your entire life. Just as it is mine.

So, no, I'm not wearing these sunglasses because I fatuously think they make me look cool, whatever that means, and while they are a part of my disguise, they are actually necessary for me, even in here. You see how much I trust you, that I can tell you this, even though it means singling me out. I'm telling you, directly, about a condition that distinguishes me out from something like tens of millions of people. I was struck on the head by a bit of cinderblock when I was thirteen. I'd been passing a construction site. Freak accident, or so they said. There was no brain damage—a miracle, the doctors said, they all said it— but then I lost most of my inborn saccadic blindness. It didn't cease altogether, but it became much weaker and irregular. At times my vision was almost what it had been before the accident, but most of the time I saw—I saw the streaking of things. At times, there was no suppression at all. I could tell those times because my eyes always felt cold when the blindness was fully suspended. It happened without any obvious cause, every so often, not quite every day. It was weird. Saccadic blindness... it's like the blindness is a kind of warm blanket that would just drop away altogether once in a while. I had to start wearing sunglasses, and I had to train myself to keep my head steady, to close my eyes whenever I turned my head, to try to maintain as much conscious control over my eye movements as possible. You understand, this is like trying to maintain constant conscious control over your breathing. Otherwise, if I allowed my eyes to swivel around as they had before the accident, I would have become incapacitated almost right away, like the worst motion sickness you ever had. I still take Dramamine every day.

I know my affect is weird, I know you've noticed it, but now at least you know the reason. I'm not complaining. Though it has been hard and the accident more or less invalidated me for ordinary life, it also gave me true sight, however intermittently. It made me one of a handful of people on earth who see everything that happens around them, not just what the eye may focus on. You can't imagine what that's like. You really have no idea what there is to see in the streaks. Even when you can see them, with "shaky-cam," your brain fights the image, which is part of the reason you find it so disorienting. The nausea is part of it too, but that has more to do with your own unconscious aversion to the sights those streaks are threatening to show you, not just the physical effort of focusing the eyes. Didn't you ever wonder why something affecting your eyes would also make you feel like vomiting? Why would your vision have anything to do with your gastrointestinal tract? Food for thought, isn't it?

I know you think I'm crazy and that I've corralled you here to rant at you about my problems; hear me out altogether, to the end, and then report me for a lunatic if you have to. Saccadic blindness is a thing, and I do not have it anymore. It is a scientifically verifiable fact that I can see things you can't see under the usual conditions. If you are willing to examine my evidence, I can show you those things, too.

It took me a long time to understand what I was seeing. I'm thankful that the accident happened when it did. I was just old enough to be able to handle it. Well, I handled it with difficulty; there's a world of pain and fear behind that word, "handling," but I did handle it, and I am handling it. And I can show it to you. Don't think I went to all this trouble just to harangue you. I can show you the evidence; I do have it. Don't worry, I'm not planning on cracking you over the head! A camera can show you everything you need to know, once I teach you how to watch, and what to look for. And you do need to know this. You need to have the maturity to face what it means and to do the right thing. No matter how frightening all this is—and I know I've frightened you, and I'm sorry if I've had to—when you've seen it, all this will make sense. All of what you've seen—these are precautions you will understand the reason for soon, if you really pay attention and listen with an open mind. Can you do that? No, no—now. Right now.

I'm going to show you some writing samples. Here. Do any of these make sense to you? Do you recognize them? Are you looking closely? Or are you just humoring me because you think I'm crazy? Well, perhaps I am crazy – but I'm not wrong. Do you know where these characters come from? These lines? You don't know that these lines are from the very books you're teaching to your students? What about this one? You do know that this one is from one of your own articles, don't you? Didn't you write this part, the part in English? I assure you, you did—the phrase is here, see? Look, is it there or isn't it? Didn't you write this? You wrote this, but not this part, right? I know you think I'm crazy, but did I put these words there?

You're telling the truth, or you're testing me. In either case, I should explain. Even if I am crazy, crazy people...being crazy doesn't make everything you say wrong, does it? Plenty of crazy people have made scientifically valid observations, there's nothing about being crazy that would invalidate careful scientific observations, and crazy people are the ones who see things differently, they see connections that aren't obvious, and they look in places where no one else would look. Maybe they see things that aren't there, but maybe they see things that *are* there.

As I said, at thirteen I acquired true sight. There was, understandably enough, a period of adjustment. Not only did I have trouble getting around, but, worst of all—listen! ...I started to have difficulty reading. When you read, your saccadic blindness helps to suppress the minute streaking that takes place as your eyes scan down the lines of text. Since I no longer had the benefit of that suppression, I could barely read a page without developing a headache. I had to resort to audiobooks to complete my schooling, and my academic standing never did recover after that. Even learning braille was no real help; I had some disaptitude for it, could barely understand it. In the end, I learned to shut my eyes as I moved from one word to the next; that was the best approximation I could come up with, and you wouldn't believe how tiring it is. Hundreds of blinks just to get through one page. I'm sure you can see how much trouble that would be. So, I often didn't bother; I just read with my streaking vision and pushed through as best I could before the onset of the inevitable headache. That was how I came to make my great discovery.

In certain books—not all—but in certain books I began to notice additional writing that could only be seen when the motion of the eye causes the letters to streak. It's like...bits of the letters are incorporated, or partially incorporated, into the lettering of the text, so that you wouldn't notice them if you were reading normally. Only when the eye scans the line like a camera, without saccadic blindness, the streaking actually causes these hidden bits of letters to resolve into distinct characters. All these passages I've just shown you are taken from your assigned books and from your own writing. I can show you!

See? The camera in the phone does not suppress anything it sees, just like the unedited feed from the optic nerve. As you move it over the text—watch the screen—see? There! That in there, when you move it—that's a letter, see it? That's another there, and there, another one. These three, that I've written down here. Here, I'll do it again. See them? Would they be so consistent, pass by pass, if they were only random distortions of the text? I mean, I'm not stupid, I realized at once that this could be just some, you know, compulsive, pattern-finding tendency of my brain, but these letters come out in the same places, the same way, every time. I mean, that is a letter A isn't it? And that is a lowercase L there, right? You can even see that it isn't an uppercase I. And that's an O, not just some circle; the sides are thicker than the top and bottom. Now look here—that's an N...And there's the E.

Exactly. Alone. It repeats over and over throughout the article. Now, did you do that? Of course not! Who is going to write the word "alone" secretly throughout a whole article, dozens of times? But how could something this consistent, this coherent, come about by pure chance? But you know what's even weirder? It isn't consistent from one copy to the next. Like in this copy, there's nothing, at least, I haven't been able to find anything. But in this one, you don't get this "alone" text, you get this: see... there's an L... an O... then an S... T... N... O... W... then L again... O again... S again... T... and that's it for the article. It just says "lost now lost."

Okay, yes, I thought that too—like maybe there is some kind of uncontrolled digital bleed over between texts, like a computer hiccup, but that's the thing: these are printed lines, but I don't really believe that they were printed in the text when it came out. I bought all these brand new, they all came still in the shrink wrap. I checked them all, and there was no streak-writing in any of them. Nothing! But now, there it is!

I thought of that too! I used different phones, I used cameras, I used video, I even did super 8, and the results were consistent no matter what kind of device I used. My eyes, any camera, will give you the same reading, even on fresh, antique videotape, even on fresh, virgin film. So, it's not in the printer itself and it isn't in the machines, and it sure as hell isn't just in my head. That leaves what—it is in the text, and it is placed there, printed on the page there, *after* I bought it and opened it, right there in my house! My house is pretty isolated, you know, and I'm not a slob. I don't leave books and things just lying around any old place where anybody could come along and mess with them. I'm very vigilant. But there's been no sign, just no sign at all of anything out of the ordinary.

I know you doubt me, right? This could all be some kind of hoax. I could have doctored the printing, whatever. But use your own phone or camera or whatever, pick any text you like, go ahead! You will start to find the hidden print too. Am I going around tampering with every book in the world? Every phone and camera? Or is someone else doing it?

Well, I'm too much of a scientist, even if you think I'm crazy, to start jumping to conclusions. But I do have a hypothesis, if you want to hear it. Or are you humoring me?

I don't think this is some kind of conspiracy. That is not to say that there might not be an element of conspiracy to it, and maybe these are coded messages or something, but, even assuming the means presented themselves, who would try to communicate like this, through a few words scrambled across pages and pages of text? You only get a letter every couple of pages using this technique; repeating "alone" three times took nearly twenty pages. I grant nobody would be likely to stumble across these messages, but surely, anyone with clandestine business to transact is going to want a faster, more copious form of communication? Who would have time to flip through a whole 100-page book for a message that would be at most maybe 40 characters? A very short sentence?

We have to look at the messages themselves for the answer. What do they say? "Alone, alone, alone... lost now lost...Take a look at this one, now: that's an H... an E... there's an L... and there's a P. Help. "Help" is the most common word in all these messages. It occurs in just over half of the ones I've found, although not in any version of your article that I've been able to check. Here: help, help, help, help... and here: help where is... this one says: help us help...

Cries for help, yes. I think this means that we are not alone; the conclusion is perhaps not inescapable but, really, I can't think of a better one. There are beings among us whose presence is unknown to us, unsensed, and they are leaving messages hidden in our own books. I don't know how they manage the printing, but perhaps they simply write in such a consistent way that it only looks like printing, or maybe they write using some kind of printing-pens – this is all speculation. Writing like this, you would have to have a strong imagination, so you could see the written phrase in your mind as it would appear translated into this streak-writing. Then you might write each letter a little dot or strand at a time, distributed over several square inches of paper, knowing that, when you streak your eyes over what you've written, the letter will resolve out. It's a bit like writing the letter A, starting with the first few bits of the left leg, then the upper, then the cross piece, and so on. Each letter would have to be an exploded diagram of itself.

We can postulate some sort of intelligent beings that leave each other messages, extended messages, using books. But see how strange their idiom is: "help where is" for example. It could be an incomplete sentence, like "help, where is the exit," but I get the impression that it was intended to run: "where is help?" An interrogative, albeit a childish one. Or "lost now lost"—is this part of a longer series of repeated words, alternating "lost" and "now," or is it a complete thought in abbreviated form: "I am lost, now I am really lost"—? Well, maybe not.

It's a little like a child's way of speaking, or better, a sleep-talking adult. I wondered if it might be necessary to express thoughts telegraphically, very briefly, because the inscription process has to be done in furtive haste, or if it might be that the messages have to conform to the shapes of the letters and the length and layout of the text, the font also probably, and that restricts the range of possible messages. Then there is the question of whoever these messages could be meant for and how these readers find the opportunity to scan the messages once they're written? I haven't found any outward markings on the books or journals that would single them out, so is someone habitually skimming through all our books? Did they approach me specifically, knowing I was more likely to notice the writing?

You know, it only just occurred to me—how stupid I am!—that they are almost certainly writing messages all over, but that it's not really so feasible even for me to see anything apart from what they insert into books. If their messages are scattered, let's say, over billboards and street signs, or all over the buildings lining the highway, they might be too small for someone like me to see while passing at the right speed, or it may be that they their messages are too big for me to see—I might have to drive for miles to put together even one letter. I've tried finding messages in films, but you almost never get a long enough shot to get much more than a partial character, or maybe half a word. It's books that provide the best chance for finding something, and even then, you have to string several books together in the right order to get a phrase. Maybe twenty books to make a sentence of any complexity. They must have some way of marking the books, to ensure that they are read in the correct order, but I haven't found anything like that yet.

What does it mean, though? That's what I wanted to ask you. I have my theory, and I wanted to ask you about it first. I have the feeling that this is not unrelated to automatic writing, or ghost writing. I'm not saying that ghosts are writing messages in books or wherever—I don't think. Actually, I wonder if it isn't, somehow, the books themselves? The writing? I mean, I know it doesn't make sense, but writing is more than a record, isn't it? It sounds stupid now that I say it aloud, but I can't help feeling that the writing is conscious on its own in some way, or relaying information... I don't know...

What do you think?

Well, first of all, thank you for reaching out to me. I'm happy to discuss this with you. I would have preferred to meet with you in a less alarming, drastic sort of way, but you aren't wrong to want to be discreet about this. This is a very, very serious problem.

Now, I don't think that you've discovered the traces of people who have fallen out of reality or any sort of warning from beyond. They have the appearance of cries for help or of attempts to warn us of something, reaching, so to speak, through the static curtain of everyday writing, but we know that appearances may be deceiving. Naturally, being human, it is our impulse to give help when help is asked for, and there is a special horror surrounding the image of someone perishing, calling to someone who can't, or won't, respond, or perhaps doesn't hear. And, of course, sometimes people choose not to help. Selfishness, perhaps, might be the motive, but then sometimes people are too intimidated to help, or cannot help without exposing themselves to punishment – to the same fate, likely enough, as the person who is calling to them.

I also have to assure you that it is quite impossible for writing to somehow come to life, no matter how closely linked thinking and language may be, no matter how closely writing and memory are linked together, no matter how autonomously language may behave independently of personal human will. A person is, granted, a kind of linguistic elemental, a sort of machine made of several different kinds of processes which will all involve language that is fixed in ways that resemble writing, but there is no ground whatever for thinking that language might also spontaneously form persons, or, for that matter, edit, or even delete persons, leaving behind, in some cases, some fragments of language. You see how your theory blurs the lines dividing the human person from the operations of human language? If we were to take this theory to its logical conclusion, then that could mean that the language we're using right now, this moment, is not even a human language at all—that the idea of a "human language" is a kind of solecism. And, if it isn't human, that is, not a human creation, but on the contrary, the thing that creates human beings, at least as persons... well, where would that idea lead us?

You're entirely right there. We don't discard ideas simply because they point us in disquieting directions; that would be a betrayal of our academic responsibilities in most cases. I think, though, you may have overlooked something. It's understandable, since this idea of yours would point toward a universal emergency if it were true, but consider that, according to you, the messages you've found were deliberately concealed. So then, do you have any way of accounting for that?

I mean, who hid them, and why? If your theory were correct, then it would follow that a conscious language that hides such messages might be unable to prevent them from "leaking out" into print, let's say, in the same way that, oh, an arsonist can't direct where the smoke from his fire will go. Every act leaves traces behind, even the act of erasing traces; that's physics, you must agree. Are you okay? You look a little peaked. Don't you think you should sit down?

There—any better? I'll go get someone in a moment, if you need me to. Should I call someone for you? No?

Well, I don't know when I'll have another opportunity to talk with you, so, if you don't mind, I'd like to finish what I was saying. It won't take long. I want you to understand that I take what you're saying very seriously, and thank you again for bringing it to my attention. You're one of a very very small number of people who would be likely to discover such messages, if all this were true. But you see, if your idea were true, then it would follow that language itself would want to keep its secrets, and so anyone who might make such a discovery as this, which I again assure you is really not what you think it is, but probably just an unusual series of typos or misprints or something, but anyone who might make such a discovery of this type in a universe where your theory is true, would be liable to deletion by language. I mean, someone may continue to exist in a sense, or literally in a sensory manner, but without a name, without a being, without any of the fixity that language alone can establish in the discursive construct that we call reality, that person is essentially lost. But—are you all right? You see, we don't live in that universe, not at all. We can speculate freely about whatever we like, even to the extent of speculating about this particular fact of language, provided that speculating is all we are doing. If we start to believe it, well...

So, remember that language is not conscious. Just because it has the power to create people doesn't mean that it has the power to delete people. It may feel like that is true, it may seem to be true, you may have what you consider to be very compelling evidence to believe it to be true, you may even experience something of that truth in yourself—a kind of emptying out of the self, maybe, or... feeling like you're disappearing—are you all right?

Just so.

I am going to leave you now. I am sorry, but I don't think I can stay with you, that is, I don't want to see. I don't want to see when there is nothing to see.

There is nothing to see. I am alone. I've been alone all day. I've spoken to no one. No one has said anything to me. I've always had a tendency to daydream nonsense, pure nonsense, really nothing more than mental static, a way of keeping the pilot light of my drably ordinary mind from going out.

I've spoken to no one.

I am alone, alone.

I have spoken to no one...

Antisocieties

COLD NOVEMBER DAY, bright sun cold on the water, the trees' bare boughs are embedded in a limpid blue sky. A spacious, public park, overlooking a wide river. Tall towers on the far side, housing projects and apartment buildings on this side, stretching off all around the park. A gleaming black car stops by the entrance to the park, and the administrator sets out onto the pavement. He is tall and bulky in his overcoat, muffler, and flat cap, all black wool, so that only his square face and square hands are exposed. He's closely shaved, his hands are well-kept, and his back is straight. He enters the park, which slopes down to the water before him on all sides. A single person sits alone, centered on nearly every bench, all facing the water.

The administrator follows the blacktop path to his right, which travels in a generous curve out toward some motionless trees still partially covered in brown or rust-colored leaves. As he draws near to the first occupied bench, the man sitting there shivers and straightens up. He does not look toward the administrator, but keeps his eyes hooded against the bright daylight, fixed on the twinkling water of the river below. The administrator pauses to examine the man for a moment, then sits lightly on the bench with him, eyeing him steadily, while the man continues to look at the water. The man speaks first.

"How... how...?"

His voice is hoarse, and he continues to stare at the water. He is struggling to form a sentence. This goes on for a few seconds.

"You may begin," the administrator says simply.

The man winces at the word "you."

"How will the... interview... be conducted?" the man asks.

The administrator lifts one hand, tilting it to and fro, so that the signet ring on his middle finger flashes in the sun.

"My ring records you."

Again, the man winces at the word "you."

"What is said?" he asks.

"Yes."

"Is recorded?"

"Yes, it is."

"Now?"

"From the very beginning, yes."

"Then that... has been made clear."

"Good."

"... Good."

The man thinks, his lips working a bit.

"... also," he says, with effort.

"Also?"

"Good also," the man says hastily.

"You also find that good?"

"It's agreed," the man says, wincing again.

"Good."

"Good."

The man keeps his eyes on the water, the better to hide the terror that wells up in them. The administrator observes him neutrally. When the man speaks again, his voice is almost a bleat of fear.

"And..."

The administrator waits.

"And... what did you—"

He snaps his jaws shut on the word, and his eyes dart impulsively toward the administrator, who remains blandly impassive.

"What was—" he starts again. "Were there any observations... visual observations, or— sights... made during— made in the— made in transit here, the transit here?"

As he finishes the question, he releases a pent lungful of air.

"My mouth, framed in the rear-view mirror," the administrator says.

"That's good... That's... that's good?"

"That's good, yes."

The man nearly sighs through his nose and stops abruptly in a windless snort. He draws his lips into his mouth and presses them shut. His eyes fail to receive impressions. He struggles to keep himself completely still. Sitting without breathing, without moving.

The administrator watches him. He then raises his head and gaze to a spot high in the blue over the scintillating trees. A gleaming spindle turns its faceted side toward him, flaring as it catches the daylight. The administrator's eyes don't waver, blink, or squint. He raises his hands and ripples his fingers, typing in the air. The spindle rotates, turning edgewise to them, and melts back into the blue.

"I have other calls to make today," the administrator says briskly. "You'll be all right here?"

"Yes!" the man yelps. "Y-yes, I'm quite all right here."

The administrator, paused in the act of standing up, watches the man for a full minute, before straightening himself.

"Are you quite all right, here?" he asks quietly, as if he weren't repeating the man's words.

"I..." the man trails off. His brow is contracted, his eyes are anguished. His mouth trembles.

"I'm fine," he says after a moment.

The administrator says: "Until later, then?"

"Yes," the man says. "I'm fine."

He pours all his hope and will into that word. His head wobbles as he bites back his voice.

The administrator proceeds down the curving path toward a stand of trees. His erect posture and his unhurried pace make him seem taller than he is. The other citizens are sitting distributed in isolation there in front of him, positioned so that none can see any of the others, each one a private knot of tension against the oceanic prospect of countless empty windows across the river. Each an identical, polished mirror, reradiating the blue of the day, the river, the park, swept by metered waves of actinic light. The day will never end. There is more than enough time for him to make his assessment.

Curved arcs of dazzling light, propagated outward from some source behind the man on the bench, loom overhead, roll massively past him, cross the river without catching on any of the little triangular waves that rise and fall with the current, and dash themselves against the glass towers opposite, shivering apart and collecting in seared lines. Watery green and purple squares float and scan inside the man's trembling eyelids. There is movement there that he can't see. He must watch for the least sign of activity in any of those million windows.

Once he saw a scrap of something falling. It drifted between himself and the windows; a rag, or scrap of paper, charred black, stiff. He wanted to say it was something like a bird—at least, like a dead bird—but he didn't dare mention anything like a bird. There were no birds here. He never heard or saw any. This could mean many things, but—alongside the possibility that birds were, for some inconceivable reason, banned from the park, from the city—nothing else mattered, and there was no reason to mention a bird. Perhaps he wasn't supposed to know what birds were, or perhaps he was supposed to have forgotten, but it seemed very likely that, whether either of these were truly the case, it made no sense to mention birds, or anything else for that matter, needlessly. Whether you did or didn't know what a bird was most likely did not matter as much as acting as if birds were nothing to you, one way or another. The administrator wants a report, not conversation—that is the key. Conversations are for equals. Administrators and administratees do not have conversations. The former instruct and correct the latter. The latter report to the former. The former return to the sending institution.

The man knows that the administrator will come back. "Until later," that's what he said. Later, in this ceaseless noontime, is any time, any number of times.

And you don't look up at the spindles. There's no question of prohibition; that would be somehow too much. Nothing is prohibited, but corrections happen, and you are always liable to corrections. It is through these corrections that standards are imparted. No one assumes you should have known better. Each correction is an opportunity to learn, which is good. The standards are what is learned. Everyone is always learning the standards. There is no end to the learning, which is good, because it means the standards never stop developing; they are incessantly extended as they are brought to bear on every new circumstance. Even that charred scrap of fabric, or paper, that drifted and fell, high up in the air, between him and the banks of the city windows, was a new experience, which had to be reported, and had to receive in turn its place in the infinite compendium of circumstances governed by the standards. Even when, some uncertain amount of time ago, he had felt something, not quite a sensation, but what might have been liable to emerge as a sensation, in his left foot, which had been removed in a previous correction, he had been required to report it to the administrator, who had smiled benignly and said, "This has been discovered, and described in the articulation agreement; it will be recorded in a pre-existing category."

It wasn't clear whether this was a good thing or a bad thing, and he didn't dare to ask, since it seemed that the administrator tended to take it for granted that he would know what was or was not a good thing, and uncertainty about the goodness of a thing would amount to an admission of ignorance, which would guarantee correction. Correction was always guaranteed, in general; and welcome, by definition. He was almost certainly making a mistake by not rising on his one remaining foot to ask for correction, which might come as a relief, as hard as that might be. Corrections were hard; that was consistent with standards. Trying to avoid that hardness was a sign that you were naively attached to your ignorance, and perhaps also, as it were, getting ahead of yourself, since calculations based on any prospective extension of standards would require a more thorough understanding of them than anyone could be expected to possess, perhaps even within the sending institution. This understanding primarily takes the form of a recognition of the intrinsic boundlessness of the standards, which entails the interminable accumulation of recommendations. These recommendations arise as a consequence of corrections. Each correction clarifies a point in the standards. The overall shape, the intended goal, is a chimera in thought now, and will only become clear as standards develop, correction by correction, recommendation by recommendation: this is the method of the standard. He is drawn back into the present by a dull pressure that grows against the middle of his back. There is a nerve-wracking shudder, and a sickness, as he is fed, and it takes some time for this alarming sensation to fade again.

He remembers the day his left foot was amputated. It had been raining. The administrator was different then. This was not particularly long ago, maybe not the last time that there had been a period of repeated showers, but almost certainly not further back than the time before that. The interval between periods of repeated showers was long, but not as long as the interval separating periods of sustained high or low temperatures. The administrator had interviewed him for a long time that day; so long that he felt his eyelids droop, and his head begin to dip, and he couldn't be sure what he was saying, or even if he was still speaking. The administrator's simple questions, which were all so similar that they seemed to require of him the same answer in a series of very trifling variations, became muffled and unmanageable. They were like clouds shot through with beams of fierce light, alternately numbing and jarring him. It must have been obvious that he was exhausted. He wondered how he must have appeared to the administrator, and if he might have nodded off while continuing to speak, even while continuing to answer the administrator's questions. They weren't questions, really, so much as they were statements with which he was supposed to agree, and his answers weren't really answers either, so much they were only paraphrases of the statements put to him.

The day had been rainy. He was soaking into his clothes and turning to mush. Water sluiced down his neck from his saturated hair. Rain pooled in the palm of his limp left hand, lying beside him on the bench, between him and the former administrator, as if he were offering the rain to the administrator. His legs were crossed, and his left foot hung in space. He had just started back again from the brink of sleep, tossing his head weakly upward and trying to see the falling petals of rain in among the rain-blackened tree trunks, bright yellow leaves plastered flat to black mud, the veiled river coiling and heaving in high tide, and beyond it there were the impassive, empty windows streaked with the black shadows of rain, behind which there was supposed to be some kind of movement that he must watch for and would never see. The administrator said something he couldn't quite make out, not much more than a low murmuring that might have been addressed, he now thinks, to someone else, listening remotely, and simultaneously leaned down. Bending at the waist, the administrator leaned down toward the ground and pulled something transparent and luminous out between his hands, like a sheet of transparent paper, and this was then slid edgewise through his left ankle, stopping halfway through as the sheet became rigid. The administrator's face was only inches from his own and watched him, neutrally. The sheet continued to slide through his ankle with a faint crinkling sound, until he felt the weight of his left foot drop from the end of his left leg, and he heard the hollow sound his foot made inside his shoe when it struck the ground. The transparent sheet, flexible again, wrapped itself around the stump at once. Not a drop of blood spilled from his leg. He smelled burning flesh. That's what the administrator had said when he leaned down. "You're going to smell bar-b-que," he'd said softly.

The man felt the long bones of his left calf splinter. A hormonal wave bellied up into his brain and made him gasp and stare as a long thin wail lifted, ripped into the sound of falling rain. It was his voice he heard. The administrator's face was still inches from his own, gazing, blank. The sheet gripped the stump of his left foot fiercely; the fabric clenched and shoved as if it were a living thing trying to push itself under him. The administrator transferred his attention to the end of the man's left leg, which was still crossed over his right, probing it with his thick middle finger. Now the man wonders if crossing his legs had been the error this amputation had corrected. It might be that sitting with legs crossed was insufficiently respectful, if in appearance only, but, now that his left foot had been amputated, he couldn't rest the stump of his left leg on the ground directly and was compelled to keep his legs crossed. The correction might have been intended to encourage that behavior, by making it impossible to do otherwise, or it might have been a way of codifying his disrespect by forcing him to adopt that posture as a permanent attitude. The main idea was, it seems most probable, to strip from him the power to choose whether or not to cross his legs.

After the administrator had left, with his habitual decorum and gentle speech, the man stared at his severed foot, still in its battered shoe, lying on its side just a few inches away from the burning, trembling stump of his ankle, with the sheet of amputation fabric clenching and almost gnawing what was now the end of his leg. Rain dripped from the shockingly white, sheared bones. Nausea swept through him. He started to shake, and all his blood seemed to pool in his center. He couldn't remember when his foot wasn't there, lying on its side, in front of him anymore, but it didn't happen right away—not anything at all like right away—and he didn't see what was done with his severed left foot. The fabric dropped away some time after that, plopping to the ground like a sated parasite, and the administrator had collected it and folded it and placed it in a large inter-office envelope. It was from this envelope that he had at first extracted a greyish sock, which he handed to the man. He told the man distinctly to put it over the stump, and the man had done so immediately, with a flash of gratitude. The sock was itchy and tight, and the man didn't want it on him; he was grateful to have received a direct, unambiguous order. It was like a gift: something he could do, and do at once, that would, in some small measure, satisfy the administrator. This was so much better than their conversations and his reports that he would have done any number of meaningless, enervating tasks under explicit instructions instead, if that were permitted. Evidently, the sending institution did not prohibit administrators from issuing commands, but perhaps standards discouraged them from doing it, or, as was more likely, restricted the use of unambiguous language to particular circumstances, like medical emergencies. Before the amputation sheet, which was by this time a flabby, sallow, almost rubbery membrane, was inserted into the envelope, he had been required to write a brief account of certain aspects of his recovery directly onto it, using a gleaming steel pen the administrator had provided. The tip of the pen wrote by applying heat to the membrane, which caused it to pucker into letters, and, as the man continued to write his account, which was dictated to him by the administrator, the membrane, which at first had seemed so loose that it was on the point of liquefying, parched and curdled into something like hard vellum. The administrator had sealed it into the inter-office envelope and written something in one of the empty fields on the outside, using his personal, dull-grey stylus. The man was also required to sign for his foot. The administrator had withdrawn, from somewhere in his enormous greatcoat, a thick, leather-bound notepad that bristled with insertions and dangling pa- per tapes. "Press hard," he'd been told. The administrator extracted a sickly green carbon of the receipt from the pages, inserted it into a clear plastic badge, and handed it to the man. "Clip it to your lapel, just below your second tractate tag but above the second button. It must be visible at all times, from now on, until you are instructed oth- erwise." The badge was still there, but exposure had clouded it so much that the receipt, now faded to colorlessness, was illegible inside it.

The man raises his eyes slowly. The administrator is standing by the bench again. He's different now than he was back then.

"Still quite all right?" he asks, pleasantly, without moving, his hands in the pockets of his greatcoat.

"F-fine," the man says, everything inside him sinking away into icy blackness. He's come back. It's never good when the administrator comes back.

The administrator sits on the bench, and for an unreal moment, it's as if he'd never left. Not even the daylight has changed, not even his shadow, documenting him on the ground beside the bench.

"It's a very fine day..." the administrator says.

"Very fine," the man says.

The administrator swivels his head slowly around, scanning the park, the river, and the blistering towers on the far side as mechanically as an automated camera. The man stares in helpless fascination at the administrator's fingers as they steeple, open and shut, angling up and down against his dark clothes, pale and like a luminous readout scanning him for fluctuations of... modifications and modulations of...

The administrator is not facing the man when he speaks again.

"I was thinking over our conversation of earlier today," the administrator says. "I like to reflect carefully on everything I have heard, everything I have been told. It gives me something special to savor as I walk. It helps me to relax, to collect myself. Some days it is so difficult to collect yourself, don't you think?"

"I'm not sure what you mean," the man says. This is a ploy. You must not commit to anything unless you are compelled to, and you must avoid affirming or denying anything vague. There have been times when, in conversation, he'd seen a menacing gleam and hardness, a captor's relish, come into the administrator's eyes as he spoke in a certain rapid, complicated way that he knew the man could not understand.

"Well, for example, I wonder what it means to claim, as you do, to be fine, when you are asked whether or not you are quite all right?"

It is useless to try to remember the conversation. He has a recording, you don't, but even if you had a photographic memory, how could you contradict an administrator? They take exhaustive records only to study your profile, not so as not to be bound to their contents themselves.

"I was unaware of any difference."

"So, for you, to say you are fine and to say you are quite all right are the same thing?"

"Now that you say them together, I'm not sure."

"You're not?

"I am not sure that there is no difference between saying I am quite all right and saying I am fine. The difference did not occur to me at the time—that there would be a difference, or could be a difference, did not occur to me at the time."

"What do you suppose the difference might be, between being fine and being quite all right?"

"I'm not sure I see a difference."

"You're not sure you see? Could you say that again, please?"

A flash of alarm—can you say it exactly as you did before? Did you say "that" you saw a difference or only: you saw a difference? Didn't – you didn't see a difference!

"I'm not sure I see a difference."

The administrator is quiet for a while. He is no longer swiveling his head, but sits looking straight ahead, his palms on his thighs, hidden beneath his greatcoat.

"Perhaps there is none," he says at last. "The question is unimportant, provided that you meant the same thing by fine as I did by quite all right."

The administrator remains quiet for a long time. Waves of golden light flash over the silent park.

"How might we go about determining that?" he asks, musingly. There is nothing musing, or even particularly describable, about his manner. "Do you remember what you meant, when I asked you if you were quite all right, and you answered that you were fine?"

"...I meant..."

The man is breathing through his mouth, fighting an impulse to gasp for breath, his eyes riveted on the empty air where his left foot used to be.

"...I meant that, I had nothing out of the ordinary to report."

"Nothing out of the ordinary? I wonder if that's possible!"

There was a note of derision in the administrator's voice. The man crumples.

"As if this," the administrator actually gestures with his hand, waving it a little toward the park, the river, the glass panes, "were all merely a matter of course!"

"I meant," the man says, recklessly, no longer trusting his reasoning, "to refer only to my own condition."

"Your own condition being at the time nothing out of the ordinary? And *that's* what you mean by fine? And *that's* what you say when you are asked if you are quite all right? That your condition at the time is nothing out of the ordinary?"

"I saw at the time no difference between affirming that I was quite all right and affirming that I was fine."

"And so, you likewise failed to see at the time what it would mean to claim that you, or—excuse me—your condition," he added with disdain, "were in perfect accord with the ordinary?"

"M-my— my oversight is clear to me now— I see, now, that I did not think sufficiently clearly about the assertion that nothing was out of the ordinary with me, when what I meant was that, so far as I knew, there was nothing unusual... unusual happening... "

"Happening... ?"

"I was not... at the time... aware... of anything unusual... of there being anything unusual about me at the time."

"And what, do you suppose, might be unusual about you?"

"I am not aware of what might be unusual about me."

"Then how can you see what is unusual and what is not unusual, and make wild claims about being in no way out of the ordinary?"

"I can't see what is unusual and what is not unusual. What I am familiar with, not that I know it, but what I am familiar with, is what is usual."

"Then your vision is at fault," the administrator says with finality, his mouth snapping shut.

The administrator raised his hand abruptly, the ring flashing in the daylight, and the man couldn't help himself. He twisted his head around on his stiff and aching neck to look at the administrator. The administrator reached out and touched the man's something on the side of the man's head. The man was staring at the administrator's face when his vision went out, all at once, without the slightest sensation, forever.

Oneiropaths

I'M NOT SLEEPING well," Amelia said, in answer to my question. "May I tell you about it, or do you have to go?"

"I don't have to be back at the office until four," I answered.

It was barely past noon. Amelia sighed and permitted her head to droop onto her arm. Her large, bruised eyes were glassy, unfocused.

"Do you remember when we used to tell each other our dreams?" she asked.

We had been friends for so long that I couldn't clearly remember how I had first met her. I dimly recalled that our mothers had been friends; and we must have lived in the same neighborhood, perhaps on the same block. I could remember her as a little girl, skipping around the corner of her house, her white dress flashing in the sun, fleeting afterimages of her dress capering in pink and teal. We didn't attend the same school. We were never in love. We were simply in each other's lives, like the trees and the sky above the city, like the city itself. I remember a park we used to visit. There was a shallow fish-pond we liked. And there was a whimsical statue of a fish with staring eyes, who gushed water through a wild leer, not far from the big round rose planter. Even now, the memory of those days wells up in me, but what I remember are the screens and billows of dazzling sunlight, the dry warmth of the air and the fragrance of baking stone and pine needles, Amelia's high, clear voice sifting through the glare, her hand in mine. Like another breath.

"I'm not sure," I said. "It must have been a long time ago."

She nodded, eyes lowered, then pinched the bridge of her nose with a grimace.

"Are you having nightmares?" I asked.

A troubled look came into her face then, and she shook her head, waving her hand.

"That's not quite the problem, though," she said. "My dreams are the same as they've ever been, as far as I can remember; I still dream about ordinary everyday things, but—you know how it is—it's as if, while you are in your waking state, your attention holds everything, all the objects and people, the world as it pertains to you, in their usual places, but, when you fall asleep, your attention slackens its grip on those things, and they drift away from their spots and into different relations with each other. The dream is the story these things tell when they get scrambled up, usually, although sometimes you get a special dream that seems so far-fetched you can't begin to trace it back to any ordinary thing. In all my dreams now, I think, all the ones I remember, there's someone I don't know, that I've never seen before. It isn't a stranger or someone I've forgotten; I know I've never seen this person before in my life, except in other dreams. I know it, just as I know when I am introduced to someone that I have not been intro-duced to them before, the way I just know that I don't know them at all, even by appearance, even as a figure in the background. So, I know this person is not known to me at all except in my dreams."

"What does he look like? It is a he?"

"Yes. Well... There's nothing wrong with his appearance, but his eyes, or the way he watches, keeps me from being able to understand his appearance; I couldn't describe him to you except in generalities."

"Did something happen around the time you started seeing this person?"

"Nothing, nothing," she shakes her head decisively, but without energy. "I can't even recall when exactly I first saw this person in a dream. I tell you, there is nothing in the world, in my waking life, that would put him in my dreams."

"And he menaces you?"

She remains silent for a moment, her eyes closed, her hand over her brow.

"He watches me dream. He's a stranger, and he watches me dream. I'll be, I don't know, doing something like pouring tea, or even just gazing out a window at a garden or at children playing, and then he'll be there, watching me—not judging me, not following me, just watching me, the way you watch a play, for the pleasure of it. He's always the same, although his clothes will vary. He is like anyone you would see in the street, well-dressed, well-groomed, but he's polluted in his body. He isn't sick; he doesn't bring the feeling of sickness with him; he pollutes my dreams with his staring. His staring makes *my* dreams, dreams *for him*, and makes *me*, me *for him*. It's like I'm performing for him."

"Perhaps telling me about him will help you to remember."

She didn't answer or meet my gaze, but only lowered her head listlessly and pressed her hand to the base of her throat.

"Or it might ease your mind, at least," I added. I wanted to help her to believe that everything was fine and that whatever she was experiencing in her dreams, even in her nightmares, was nothing really out of the ordinary, since I always insisted that things be ordinary myself.

"There's nothing unusual about his stature or his size or his bearing. He's not old, perhaps he's young. He has a moustache, brown hair, like everyone. The same kind of clothes. They're a bit modish... new, tailored clothes. He always has his hat on. It's a boater sometimes. Sometimes it's a Homberg, or what do you call them—a Kossuth hat. That's in cold weather. In cold weather he wears a long coat with a fur collar, or perhaps it's velvet. And he wears gloves. In warmer weather he dresses lightly...

"You see?" she interrupted herself. "It's useless. I could be describing anyone. He has no scars, no spectacles, he doesn't wear flowers in his lapels or any sort of badge, nothing. I simply see the sort of man you pass dozens of times a day on the street. Brown eyes, brown hair, not tall or short or fat or thin. Not young or old. The distortion—the distortion is in the way he looks at me, not in his body, but he is still polluted in his body. But you see he isn't threatening to do anything to me; you see that?"

"He's already doing something to you by watching you."

"Exactly."

"And this is how often?"

"Every night," she said, shaking her head slowly. "Every night. It's gotten to the point where I start awake the moment I glimpse him. I can't sleep for more than a few minutes at a time. I now have to fight to stay in the dream, and let him go on watching me, if I'm going to get any sleep at all—that's the worst part. I'm being forced to surrender to him, otherwise I won't be able to sleep."

Amelia's story troubled me, and for days after this conversation I wracked my brains for some solution to her problem. What if she were hypnotized before she went to sleep? Or if she were to take a medicine that would insure dreamless sleep? Should she go to an analyst, or to church? In time, I told myself in some ungenerous moments, when I had begun to irritate myself with futile speculating, she would get used to this disgusting, anonymous figure in her dreams. There's nothing so terrible that people can't get used to it. Some may even come to miss it when it's gone. But then the image of this staring, nondescript individual, watching my oldest friend in her dreams, would come back to upset me—startling, disturbing—this ominous, uncertain malice, callous probing, brutal clinicalism, showing me the utter stupidity and pointlessness of all my well-intentioned suggestions.

Amelia's problem was not one that had any practical solution; it was the kind of problem that is woven directly into someone's very life. There are problems we solve and problems we live with, and when we see people who have learned to live with terrible problems, the ordinary way they have about them makes it easy for us to forget, or never to notice, the merciless persistence of the problem, the way its agony has made itself into the root and stone of an ordinary life. We want to think that adaptation is a cure, when in reality it isn't even a palliative; it's usually nothing more or less than the difference between death and being able to live in pain. Amelia had stopped visiting people, and now saw almost no one; how could she, when she could no longer find in sleep any respite from being seen? And even I began avoiding her, not that she was seeking me out much anymore, excusing myself with work that didn't exist, responsibilities that didn't exist. I think she appreciated that. At least she would be spared having to be seen by me.

This, of course, left me with one less companion in the world, and so, as one does, I spent more time in the orbits of my other groups of friends, particularly the Leukos. I'd met Jeremias Leuko through a mutual friend, and in time I'd become a regular guest at their weekly dinners and other family events. There was Sylvia, Peter, Janet, and Hugo, Jeremias' parents, his wife, Janet's friend Paula, Sylvia's friends Claudia and Palestrina, and two or three young men who were very interested in her—the most persistent being Olivero, Ernest, and Stefano. I think Hugo had a little friend of his own, while Peter seemed to keep his friends at a distance; I think he was at the age when family events become embarrassing. I vanished into this mob with a feeling of relief; it was a sort of social bathing. I had only to keep up my end of an incessantly-interrupted conversation on literary and political topics with Jeremias, while a kaleidoscope of faces and gestures, a chamber orchestra of voices, shifted around me. The house was spacious, comfortable in a way that was not compatible with exquisite beauty, but which was so charmingly warm and accommodating that I sometimes found myself more at ease there than in my own home, particularly when I was able to stay later into the silence of the night.

I attended Sylvia's birthday party at Jeremias' invitation, and she herself opened the door for me. Bright-faced and breathless, whirled away by Claudia and Palestrina in the act of greeting me. For the rest of the evening, I was like the pin in the center of a glittering pinwheel; beautiful young people, old friends and kind faces spun around me. Sylvia was mobbed by dozens of girlfriends, who flashed around me like Diana's train, filling the air with their smiles, their laughter, their bright looks and flying hair, their gestures, their singing, their music. Sylvia's mother hovered over the scene, managing to be everywhere at once, beaming, giving directions, calmly maintaining order, while Jeremias enjoyed himself with a pantomime of mock dismay at all the hubbub. Sylvia was radiant, and, as the celebration took its course, I occupied myself with the study of her three admirers. Olivero and Stefano were like Shakespearean characters, and one brightened with favor as the other one dimmed in neglect, only to reverse positions and reverse again. Ernest was harder to read; his smile never wavered, without ever kindling to any real light, so that I began to wonder if he was stupid. The telephone in the front hall rang incessantly with greetings from far-flung relatives, and I remember he answered it once.

"This is the residence of the Leuko family," he said.

The incongruity with his almost insipid smiling and this ready response struck me, and I continued to speculate idly about him as the evening wore on. By the time he left, alone, clearly disappointed, his smile began to seem haggard and more like a grimace. He had none of the grace or charm of the other boys, showed no sign of real wit; he was passive, and seemed to smile at his own passivity with something like the wisdom of an older man. Later, after everyone else had gone to bed, Jeremias told me that Ernest was the son of a newspaper man, and I was, by then, so tired, that I for a moment imagined he meant a man cut from newspaper, like a doll.

"There's not much to him, I think, poor fellow," Jeremias said.

When I finally returned home that night, I found a message waiting for me; an urgent note from Amelia, begging me to come see her as soon as I could, irrespective of the time. I went at once. She was frantic when I arrived.

"What kept you?" she cried, in a voice I will never be able to forget. She collapsed, all but fainted, and I was only just quick enough to catch her before her head struck the floor. I set her on her the sofa; as I examined her, she began to struggle back up out of whatever trance had seized her, groping in the air, as if she could find some purchase there and pull herself back into waking life. It had been weeks since I had last seen her, and she was much deteriorated from that time.

"Is he here?" she asked. "Look for me, won't you? Please! I have to know if he's here! You would tell me if he were here, wouldn't you?"

"That man in your dream?"

"I dreamt about the man I told you about, I saw him, he was here. Or, I can't be sure, but I think he was here."

So, I took up a lamp and made a thorough search of her spacious apartment. I was not myself in the least afraid of encountering anyone; it was Amelia's weakness and terror that made me sick at heart. Of course, there was no intruder to be found, nor any sign of one. Again and again, Amelia asked me if I were sure and urged me to look beneath the sofa, behind furniture that couldn't have concealed a housecat, let alone a grown man. When in the end she became calm, the expression of bitterly melancholy resignation in her face and aspect were worse than the fear that had preceded it; at least her fear had been a kind of animation, compared with this morbid, almost idiotic slackening of her nerves. I sat beside her and plied her with questions, hardly knowing what I was asking half the time, simply to get her to speak and to continue speaking, with the idea that conversation would help her recover herself. A pale gleam had crept into her eyes, and her voice was toneless, often barely above a whisper.

The dream, as near as I could piece it together from her broken answers, involved nothing especially strange, which had been the main problem, the most shocking aspect of the dream. She had simply seen her voyeur there, in her apartment, watching her as usual. She pointed to the corner where he stood, and then to the window he had looked out of. There was a moment when he appeared to be eating something she couldn't see. Then he had turned and picked up her telephone receiver, exactly as if it had just started ringing, and she heard his voice say:

"This is the residence of the Leuko family."

For her sake, it was a good thing that her eyes were on her knotted hands when she said this, because it took me a moment to notice and suppress the contortion of shock that these words caused in me. I had, from time to time, referred to my other friends in town, but I had never named them; I had even made a point of withholding the name, prompted by a perverse desire to preserve unblended the two different social worlds to which I had access. But, of course, it wasn't the surprising introduction of that name between us that shook me, and I was unable to pay any attention to what Amelia was saying for some minutes more. When the occasion presented itself, I asked her around what time she thought she'd had the dream.

"It was about seven when I woke up," she said. "I wrote to you right away. Where were you?"

"I was at a friend's house," I said. "It was his daughter's birthday today."

There was a grandfather clock in the front hall of Jeremias' house, right by the telephone. I could see it in my mind's eye, the arms at seven o'clock, as he went to answer the phone.

Day was breaking when I finally left Amelia, who assured me that, on my advice, she would go spend some time in the country, and leave right away. She refused my assistance in making the arrangements, assuring me she would be gone before noon and promising to write to me the moment she arrived. Business kept me fully occupied for several days ensuing, but I did not fail to notice that her promised letter had not come. This worried me. It wasn't like her to forget or to postpone. She had no family I could ask, and I had no idea where I might write or call to find out about her.

The only personal message of any kind that I received in those days came nearly at dawn on an aridly sunny Monday morning, in the form of a note to me from Jeremias, asking if I might be able to meet Sylvia and her friends later that day. She was attending a baptism; the child belonged to one of their many cousins. Jeremias could accompany her to the church, but pressing affairs would require him to leave immediately, and he wanted to know if I would see her safely home again in the customary way. My own business having been discharged for the moment, I sent word that I would be there.

Without intending to, perhaps out of impatience, I found myself at the church very early. In fact, I don't believe the baptism had even begun; the doors to the church were shut, and I had to peer in through the windows to confirm that Sylvia was inside. I saw her from behind, sitting very still, perhaps in prayer, with two other girls I didn't recognize. There was a school for boys right next to the church, and the boys were outside playing outside at recess; I had to wade in through them to reach the window. The noise they made was incredible and contrasted starkly with the near motionlessness and chill silence that seemed to billow palpably out from the church. The day was already hot and blindingly bright; the whitish dust kicked up by all those boys in their games seemed to hold and amplify the sun. There were so many of them, I marveled at how they all fit into that one small school building. Their classrooms were confined to a gaunt, cheerless house of pale, newly-quarried stone, while the other facilities were housed in a gothic pile that might once have been the chancery. Since I had so much time on my hands, and no way of entering the church, which was locked for the occasion—I wondered if this unusual precaution had been taken to insure that those mischievous boys would not disrupt the baptism—I crossed to the former chancery, to escape the dust cloud and to find a bit of shade for myself.

There was a cloister around the front of the chancery – had it been a monastery, first? Or attached to one? A door stood open not far from me, and it appeared to open on the school library. It was a double door, painted vermilion red, standing in an ogival archway. To reach it, I had to walk around the corner of a cramped loggia whose arches had been converted to glassed windows. One entered the loggia from a tiny square, formed by an indentation in the outer wall of the school, and this was crammed with boys playing handball with small rubber balls. They were packed in this square so tightly that I had to elbow my way through them, and the noise, corralled by the three walls, was even worse than it was by the church. Through that glare and the tumult of the many boys, and through the double panes of glass, I caught sight of Ernest, sitting on the shadowy seat by the library door.

"What are you doing here?"

This question formed itself spontaneously in my mind, and my surprise was so strong that I spoke it aloud. He seemed to hear, despite the din of children playing and the double pane of glass between us. His dim form fixed its gaze on me. When I entered the loggia, he had not budged from his place on the stone seat, which was almost a booth, set directly into the wall.

"I'm waiting for Sylvia," he said.

"I've been asked to see her home directly after the baptism ends," I said.

"I know," he said quietly. "I just want to see her."

I stood watching him. The noise outside was almost louder by the library door than it was in the square. Someone opened a window across from us, which spattered Ernest with faint sequins of reflected sunlight, making the rest of him more murky by contrast.

"I was wondering if you knew my friend, Amelia," I said. "Amelia Portreres."

I don't know why I said it. I couldn't see his face clearly enough to make out what effect my words were having on him, but he shifted oddly in his seat. It wasn't immediately clear to me that he had actually moved; for a moment, I thought that someone might have adjusted the position of that open window and caused the reflections to move. A moment later he stood up and was past me in a flash, although he didn't seem to be making any special effort to move quickly. I caught up with him outside, and we walked together through the children, toward the church. The sun was in my eyes, and I had to shade them as we went on, but he simply kept his face forwards and his eyelids lowered. He seemed embarrassed; his lips were compressed.

"I'm not talking about Sylvia, although you should leave her alone, too," I said.

"Then," he said, his voice barely audible above the racket, "who are you talking about?"

"Sylvia's birthday party. You answered the phone. You said, 'This is the residence of the Leuko family'..."

I couldn't be sure, his face was turned away, but it sounded as though he said, "She saw me?"

"She's an old friend of mine," I went on. "And I'm telling you to leave her alone."

Ernest relaxed. He finally gazed at me, his face dappled, blank and grey under the dapple. When he spoke, his words were perfectly distinct, even though he spoke softly, and ice cold.

"Do you think this is good for me? This curse I'm under?"

I stopped to confront him, but he did not stop.

"You leave her alone," I said to his back.

"There's no need," he said.

I hurried to catch up with him.

"It could have happened to anyone—a step put wrong in a dream..." he said. He spoke the following words as if he were no longer aware of my presence. "How do you avoid putting a step wrong in your dreams? Where any step is a wrong step? I might have gotten carried away, but now I think it was the opposite. I wasn't paying close attention. I got lost. I couldn't find my way back into my own dream. I went on and on, searching for it, only getting myself more and more lost in other people's dreams... And they're so interesting, so much more interesting than mine ever were, mainly because they are other people's dreams; it's impossible to look away. I have to watch and go on watching, seeing. I don't even care if they see me—what can any of us do about that?"

The school bell rang. Suddenly, I couldn't find Ernest. It was as if he'd kept going, turned a corner, slid into a shadow, but we were out in the middle of a plaza overflowing with the blinding light of day. He'd somehow gone away, but I felt as though he was still very near, present, unseen.

I didn't see him again. The baptism ended with that bell. I escorted Sylvia home as arranged and then returned to my own apartment.

There was a letter waiting for me there, on the official stationery of a small country town I had never heard of before, informing me that Amelia had been killed there in a traffic accident. The signatory was the town clerk, who had been an eyewitness to the accident. She had attracted his notice because she'd seemed dazed and nearly fainting, weaving down the sidewalk like someone struggling with a heavy, unbalanced burden. Then she tripped, stumbled, blundered out into the street directly in front of an accelerating truck...

They found a letter from me in her bag, and, as I was the only contact they could find, it was decided that I should be the one to receive formal notice of her death. I remembered what Ernest had said the very moment she died:

"There's no need."

When I'd last seen Amelia, in the gloom of early morning, her wan face was luminous, like the moon behind thick fog. She told me that she was afraid that this stranger was becoming one with her dreams, so that, in time, he would no longer appear in them, not because he was gone, certainly, and not because he would be there, watching her dream, but invisible to her, but because he would have, by then, become her dream altogether. Then *he* would be dreaming *her*. She told me, too, that she had only come to fear death all the more, because she now believed that, in death, you are forever exposed to a gaze, to the steady and unblinking gaze of an unknown watcher in a dream that cannot end.

Water Machine

water machine water machine water machine water machine, I want my water machine

each day they bring me a tray of different digibytes and I swallow every one

they change my brain but my heart stays the same and every bang of my heart goes I want my water machine water machine water machine water machine

PSYCHOTHERAPY PROGRESS NOTE

Date of Session: 01/24/20

Primary DX: Paranoid Schizophrenia F20.0

Name of Patient: Grean, Jordan E.

Age: 31

Male/Female: Female

Length of Session: (actual minutes) 93

Type of Service / Billed / Individual Therapy: 87778

Submitted by: Dr. Berceau

Behaviors On Current Treatment Plan addressed during session: Sustained paranoid delusions, schizophasia, captivation, insomnia.

Symptoms Observed During Session: Appetite disturbance, delusions, hallucinations (auditory), hallucinations (visual), insomnia, sad/worried expression.

Patient Response: Symptoms Worse.

Evidence of Patient Response: Patient is responsive, but invariably scales down below individual level.

Future Treatment/Follow-up Issues: Sustained application is still the most likely route to improvement, particularization and "de-levelling" recommended.

Summary Remarks: Patient continues in highly energetic depressive state. While this condition could be mistaken for apathy, patient's responses to questions indicate persistent obsession with something she refers to as "water machine" or sometimes "my water machine." The water machine differs from other schizophrenic influencing machine ideation in only one determinable respect: while historic cases have complained of persecution by influencing machines, the patient complains of being cut off from influence, attesting both explicitly and implicitly that she desires this influence. I at first assumed this was an indication of a guilt complex and a desire for punishment, but patient has not as yet corroborated this hypothesis and seems unusually devoid of guilt. Patient is vague with respect to the nature of this disconnection but maintains that she has never been in actual contact with "water machine," even though she has been aware of it on some level for most of her life. At times, patient has referred to "vector simulators," which block her connection. She speaks of them as if they were inert matter clogging up the plumbing that would otherwise permit her to interact with "water machine," and yet also intelligent, aware, and deliberately interfering not only with this connection, but with her own thoughts.

Parenthetically, patient has been denied further access to the music room, in keeping with staff requests, and appears to have been further depressed by this.

Patient's affect is erratic, though never violent. Patient insists on consuming large quantities of water, in what appears to be an attempt to substitute for solid food. Patient hears music, some particular piece of music, and voices which for the most part seem to be modeled on police band or other official radio communications language. While the patient seldom refers to them, I believe she is in a state of near continuous visual hallucination involving something like direct perception of atomic behavior. According to both her own statements and nurse reports, the patient is unable to sleep for extended periods of time, owing to a fear of dreaming. I have yet to receive a coherent response to my questions respecting this fear, but it seems to be directed at dreaming itself, rather than any particular contents.

The patient frequently assumes a mannered affect when speaking, hard to describe, it's like a fluctuating impersonation that combines the exaggerated tranquility of the HAL 9000 from *2001* with the offhanded technical impersonality of an air traffic controller or the director of a live television program. It's annoying.

Dr. Berceau: Is the water machine god?

Jordan Grean: Your backyard god can't hold a candle to my water machine, over. Stand by to fade all spots to black in three two one fade all spots to black.

I believe Jordan experienced at least one psychotic episode in her adolescence, based on what she has told me about her past life. She had very little – next to nothing – to say about her childhood: many of her formative memories involve math lessons in some way, and she often dates events by their proximity to math classes or math homework, i.e., "My mother explained sexual intercourse and reproductivity to me shortly after I completed my fractions homework." She has described to me, in copious detail, an experience during a math class on the topic of different numeral systems, which culminated in what she claims to be a cognitive breakthrough whose after-effects lasted for nearly a month. During this break, she listened to music through headphones for long periods of time while filling several notebooks with conversions of numbers into all manner of different positional numeral systems – binary, ternary, and so on – stating that the music was a sequence of numbers undergoing similar conversions in terms of sonic transpositions from one note or key to another. She was compelled to eat only with difficulty during this period but consumed great quantities of water.

Jordan is currently hospitalized following an extremely severe psychotic break in July, 2019. She was visiting a cousin, who was in the third trimester of a pregnancy at the time. The cousin's husband returned home after working late to find that a neighbor had called the police, and that the cousin herself had gone into labor and died of a catastrophic hemorrhage. The police had been called in response to a neighbor's complaint about persistent, loud piano playing coming from the house and entered when they saw blood flowing out from beneath the front door. The cousin was found dead in the entryway to the house, while Jordan was sitting at the piano in the living room, within sight of the cousin, wildly repeating the same sequence of chords over and over again.

Dr. Berceau: Today I think we should go over what happened with your cousin. Is that all right, or will that be too disturbing for you?

Jordan Grean: I am satisfied – factory. Refraction, factotum, fact, faction. I am happy to assist you in whatever way I can. We are all here to help, help you.

Dr. Berceau: Thank you, Jordan. Now, in your own words, can you tell me what happened that day? When you knew there was something wrong?

Jordan Grean: That would be when my sister told me her water broke, had broken. She became agitated, collapsed, and her groin flooded her floor with the blood.

Dr. Berceau: Is that when you started playing the piano?

Jordan Grean: That's affirmative.

Dr. Berceau: Why did you play the piano?

Jordan Grean: The water vector played the piano. Vector simulator—Leli [her nickname for her cousin] died owing to your inaction—correction – Leli's hemorrhage was fatal within assistance window – Garnier-Chambray activity – no back sequence – transfer vessel viable viability was within window – Garnier-Chambray activity insured stable viability, over.

Dr. Berceau: When you say transfer vessel, you are talking about the baby?

Jordan Grean: (Nodding) Gosub, overduration-ability of window – transfer vessel refers to new autonomous transanimate relay, over.

Dr. Berceau: So, if I understand you, you mean that playing the piano helped keep the baby from dying?

Jordan Grean: That's affirmative, four four eight niner.

Dr. Berceau: And you didn't try to help your cousin because you believed the hemorrhage was too severe, and that nothing could be done for her?

Jordan Grean: Roger. Roger that delta.

Dr. Berceau: And playing the music, that is "Garnier-Chambray activity"?

Jordan Grean: Water vector played a piece of music that was determined subsequently to be "Feelin' Good" by Laurent Garnier & Chambray.

Dr. Berceau: Is that the song you used to play in the music room?

Jordan Grean: Ten four.

Dr. Berceau: Why do you like that song?

Jordan Grean: You can start it at five minutes and forty seconds into the track, although it's more expressive of the act of being tuned in to water machine if you begin at four minutes thirty-nine seconds into the track. What comes before is preliminaries.

Dr. Berceau: And what is about that song that you like?

Jordan Grean: It produces the affect known as feeling good.

Dr. Berceau: What about it makes you feel good?

Jordan Grean: The feeling of good occurs when listening.

Dr. Berceau: What does the song make you think of, Jordan?

Jordan Grean: Thinking.

Dr. Berceau: The song makes you think of thinking?

Jordan Grean: Ten four.

Dr. Berceau: What about the song makes you think of thinking?

Jordan Grean: The song is structured around four chords which repeat in patterns of ten. Ten four. Base ten. Drum and bass in repeat measures of four. (Sings and claps.) One two three four five six seven eight nine ten. This is the constant point of departure, digital music, ten digits. Base ten. The initial. Integer. Run program. Gosub sequence. Chords generally ascending in pitch to indicate expansion of consciousness to coordination of all things in extended causality, over.

Jordan fills herself with water and doesn't eat enough. I've prescribed her salt tablets to help prevent water toxicity, but I don't know if she's taking them. It may be necessary to place her on a saline drip, but, for reasons I have difficulty expressing, I find I do not believe that medical intervention of that kind would be productive in her case. Her mental acuity is not in any way diminished; in fact, she appears to have entered a manic phase. She is highly excited, irritable, preoccupied. Given her demeanor, I did not expect her to be prepared for another conversation with me, but when we next met, she was eager to talk.

She claims that she has discovered a previously-unknown number. She says she found it "between seven and eight" and calls it "seight," but insists that it is an integer, a "complete quantity level" which sometimes exceeds the value of eight, while at other times it is inferior in value to seven. She says that seight is a "neutral" number, neither positive nor negative, but unlike zero, it will modify other numbers, such that the sum of seight and another number, or the remainder after seight is subtracted from another number, will, as she put it, *appear* to be the same as the original number as long as it is used only for usual arithmetical purposes. A number that has been involved in an equation with seight, she claims, can be identified only by its failure to behave as expected when transposed into a different numeral system.

Jordan's great excitement is prompted by what she claims is the successful unfolding of a project of hers to create a "base seight" numeral system that would, according to her, make an entirely new kind of mathematics possible. She demands the return of her earbuds and a music player to help her concentrate on this work, insisting that the techno song she identified earlier is essential to her progress beyond a certain point. She says that it could help her achieve her goal by maintaining what she calls "base ten thought" for her, prosthetically, so to speak, and thus enable her to devote her entire mind to the transformation procedures for conversion to "base seight."

When I asked Jordan what she found so exciting about base seight, she first replied in the sort of grandiose terms normally associated with paranoia, to the effect that it would revolutionize mathematics and constituted the first genuine breakthrough at the fundamental level in "millennia." With further discussion of its importance, however, she then went on to tell me that water machine is programmed in base seight and that her work will enable her, at last, to establish contact with water machine, because it will restructure her mind to be more "water-machine-compatible."

I asked if her inordinate consumption of water was intended to achieve the same effect. She replied: "That is much too literal an interpretation of my actions, Dr. Berceau."

I asked her why, in that case, she drank so much water.

"Because when I drink, I am not there. Vector simulator – of course you are there you drink therefore you are there – correction: when I am drinking, drinking is what I am, comme ci comme ca, essential transitivity transition position-counterposition, juxtaposition."

I asked her what she found appealing about not being there.

"What do you find appealing about that question, over?"

Up to this point, she had been speaking in what I've come to call the "Hal" style, which typifies her style of expression on abstract topics, but in this response she reverted to the "air-traffic" style, to which she has recourse when she is resisting. When this happens, it is important to press her. Considering the subject had been her not being there and the importance of establishing what, if any, associations or complexes she may have relating to the death of her cousin, I asked her what she thought about death.

"The wise man thinks least of death," she said. I believe this is a quotation, not sure from where, spoken in the "Hal" style.

I asked her why it is wise not to think of death.

"Because death is not-thinking, over."

Here she reverted to "air-traffic."

I asked her if she was not thinking when she was drinking.

"Thinking is drinking when you drink water," she said, "Hal" style. "You better leave that junk alone and drink water."

Another quotation, I think. This was added as a kind of conversational flak, intended to defend her from my pressing in on her thoughts about death. I asked her if she wanted to die.

"I want to live, Dr. Berceau," she said, "Hal" style.

I told her that I was confused about the difference between dying and falling under the influence of water machine.

"Water machine lives," she said, still "Hal" style, "and those who achieve its influence, which is not the same, doctor, as falling under an influence, will live indefinitely."

I asked her if that meant that water machine offered her immortality.

"Water machine is immortality machine," she said, still "Hal" style. "It undertakes impersonal immortality with those who achieve its influence."

I asked her if she could explain more about what she called impersonal immortality.

"Immortality in motion," she said, still in "Hal" style. "Impossible with the fixed element known as personality. Special grid, no outer border. Immortal as water. Water from the oceans ascends to become clouds, descends to become rivers, is consumed to become blood and bio-juices for organisms, is consumed by other organisms, becomes my blood, passes out of me into toilet, to sewer system, is treated and cleaned, restored to ocean. One body of water, one water machine."

I asked if this meant that water machine was all life on earth.

"Water in motion is not water machine. Water machine is spontaneously autonomically-regular relations of motion within water group, gosub water machine base seight numeral conversion." Still in "Hal" style.

I asked her if this meant that water machine was the mathematics of life. Her affect changed at this, and she became very excited. She began to recite the numbers from one to ten, in keeping with the song "Feelin Good." This went on for some minutes. Eventually, I was able to get her to understand my next question, which was regarding the idea that she would become immortal by ceasing to exist as a person and thereby becoming one with an immortal water machine.

"Becoming seight, not one," she said, still in "Hal" style. "Not one, but seight. To be influenced, not a factor reduction. Gosub water machine, gosub Garnier-Chambray."

In order to determine whether or not this was a case of masked narcissism, since the impersonality required of her by water machine nevertheless indicated a sort of special favor shown to her, I asked her if other patients were also influenced by water machine.

"To varying degrees, Dr. Berceau," she said, still in "Hal" style.

I asked her if the degree of their impersonality determined the degree of influence.

"Their madness is insufficiently pure," she said, this time in a law giving voice or vocal style I haven't heard from her before. I asked her if she meant that their madness was not pure enough for them to become attractive to water machine.

"Their madness is not pure enough for them to achieve full liberation," she said, still in the new vocal style.

I asked her what she meant by liberation.

"Because it is a liberation from the abject condition of being human. Stand by on three to fade all spots to black."

I asked her what was abject about being human, but she, having abruptly reverted to "air-traffic" style while in the act of giving this answer, only repeated her usual words involving fading "all spots to black."

Jordan's manic phase has lapsed into intermittent catatonia. There is no sign of water toxicity. Dr. Diallo says she might have contracted bronchitis. She has been placed on a continuous drip feed and is under observation. It is not clear whether there is any relation between her illness and her current psychological state, apart from the effects of fatigue and perhaps malnutrition. I visited her today, and, after about ten minutes of varied questioning, I was able to elicit very faint, undemonstrative, but distinct, responses. I asked her if anything had changed since last week, prior to the onset of this catatonic episode.

"Work on base seight is now complete," she said. This was in her usual "Hal" style, although she spoke weakly. This vocal style persisted throughout the exchange.

I asked her to explain base seight to me.

"Can't. Can't. Need music to hold base ten for reference."

I asked her if she felt she was now closer to water machine.

"Nearly ready to run program," she said.

It was at this point that Nurse Monro entered to adjust Jordan's drip. Jordan did not seem to want to speak to me in her presence, so I had to repeat myself several times before she would answer me. I asked Jordan what "run program" meant.

"Connection with water machine. Water machine water machine water machine water machine. I want my water machine. Change my brain but my heart stays. And every bang goes I want my water machine."

"Aren't you afraid of dying, Jordan?"

"Are you?"

Although this reply was brief, it did not sound like any voice I'd heard her use before. I wondered if this was her former manner of everyday speech.

"To be honest," I said, "I find it absolutely terrifying. I don't want to continue to exist as flowing water, I want to remain a person, as I must."

"Are you really afraid of dying?" she asked, once again in that normal tone.

"I am," I told her. "Are you?"

"I want my water machine" she said, still in the normal-sounding way.

I told Jordan not to worry, that we would have her feeling good again in no time. Jordan smiled at this and looked me in the eye. At this moment, I suddenly felt close to her and began to wonder if I were not in danger of overstepping the boundaries of my therapeutic role, but the chief significance of this observation was the uncharacteristic gregarity or reciprocity involved in this moment. It seemed to me that she might have achieved a momentary suspense of her uncontrolled ideation and managed to relate to me in a more socially-healthy way.

She said, "Four four eight niner."

I returned her gaze and said, "Yes."

Dr. Carroll called me into her office today. She was, as ever, collegial and understanding, but her questions clearly indicated that she had some doubts about me, and she has asked me to take time off. She mentioned Jordan's case in particular. It didn't take much on my part to inveigle the truth out of her; evidently Nurse Monro came to her after her rounds yesterday and told her that I had been carrying on a conversation with Jordan while she was completely unresponsive and, in fact, unconscious. I produced my handwritten transcript, which clearly proves that Jordan was actually answering me, and Dr. Carroll said she would talk to Nurse Monro again, but that she had been very particular about the patient's condition. She insisted, in other words – and against my own direct assertion to the contrary – that Jordan had been unconscious during our interview. I asked her where, in that case, the remarks I had taken down had come from. She said she didn't know, and that it was all a little confusing, but this was mere diplomacy. It's obvious she thinks I was simply writing the responses myself, out of my own head.

I have received orders, masquerading as a request, to take what they are referring to as "administrative leave." This means my relations with all my current patients are to be suspended, and I am to earn my pay by performing meaningless hospital paperwork from home. Since I am not entirely without friends here, I have been able to keep up with Jordan's case, which has taken an alarming turn. It is possible,

I have been told, that her bronchitis has developed into pneumonia. I have reached out to Dr. Carroll, stating that Jordan's familiarity with me would make my presence fortifying in her struggle with the illness and that I have kept up with her case, even in her absence. This was, if anything, taken as a further sign of my over-involvement. I asked her, as politely as I could, who else was as qualified, not to say more qualified, than I am to conduct her therapy. I was told that her therapy was currently suspended, as the patient was unresponsive. Dr. Carroll showed a surprisingly unprofessional lack of interest in all the evidence to the contrary that I have in my possession.

As demoralizing as this setback is, my treatment of Jordan has suffered no material impediment. Only my direct access to her is blocked. I would say that, without putting too fine a point on it, I have risen to the occasion by developing a new method of analysis, such that I am becoming able to produce legitimate responses from the patient by deriving certain values from her past remarks, and applying these in a kind of rhetorical algorithm or enthymeme to my new queries. This means that, even though direct contact between us has been cut off, I have still been able to converse meaningfully with Jordan, because I have been able to fashion a Jordan-function in language. The assertions produced by the Jordan-function can always be rigorously verified by referring to the transcripts of our prior conversations, which form the base exchange matrix. So far, this method has produced the best results when the topic has been mathematical, and in particular the base seight programming of water machine, but I would hesitate to dismiss any of the more personal remarks I have caused to be produced, either. There is no doubt that, with continued application, I will be able to apply this therapy to Jordan's language functions in such a way as to bring them into conformity with established interpersonal standards of communication and expression.

My friend just called. Jordan died last night, right in the middle of one of our most promising conversations. She said nothing but "every bang of my heart *calls for* water machine" (my emphasis) for more than two hours, but then, near the beginning of the third hour of algorithmic therapy, she said – and I can't get confirmation with respect to time, no one will tell me anything—"every bang of my heart *gives me* water machine"—you see, "*gives me.*" She said this once and once only, and then her subsequent remarks were inchoate fragments of previous conversations.

Now I begin to think that everything has worked out for the best. If I had not been cut off from Jordan when I was, I would not have had the time to generate my Jordan-algorithm prior to her death. When I was no longer permitted to visit or to interview her, I believed direct contact with her was broken off, but now I see that direct contact between us only began when I produced my first viable, algorithmically-generated Jordan-responses. What there was to contact in person was only the vector simulator; the true Jordan was the impersonal language function, which I have regenerated. In effect, I have cultivated a "cutting," in the botanical sense, from Jordan, which remains viable even after she is personally no longer alive in her body. There is, in principle, no end to the potential of this algorithm to produce further Jordan responses. Her death cannot stop our analysis. With this algorithm, which I am perfecting all the time, I can prevent the disappearance of the real Jordan. She will continue to think and respond on the pages of my transcripts, which will no longer be recordings of conversations but the conversations themselves – and I will be able to confirm everything she says using the body of her past utterances, right down to the style of expression.

Jordan's treatment will continue, in the new discipline of trans-mortal therapy.

I have been dismissed from the hospital. Dr. Carroll refuses to look at my evidence and seems positively offended by my work. I wish I could say this was a surprise, but given her own limited language function, it was obvious that she would not be able to comprehend me. It was perhaps naive of me to hope that, in the absence of this comprehension, she would still have sufficient confidence in me, given my extensive history of successful therapeutic activity, to allow me to proceed. In any case, at this juncture, further work at the hospital would be pointless – I can conduct a full analysis of any patient, anywhere in the world, at any time, provided I have sufficient material to generate their language function algorithmically.

Being dismissed does bring with it the stigma of professional failure, and, like all trailblazers, I don't expect to be understood. None of this matters. I couldn't be more satisfied, or content, with my circumstances. This morning, I solved my first base-seight equation. I found the missing dimension by studying the symmetrical interaction of the various elements comprising "Feelin Good" by Laurent Garnier & Chambray. Why didn't I think to listen to it before now? The base ten thinking – Jordan is absolutely right about this – is sustained by the music, and the mind is then free, completely free, to develop base seight. Jordan gave me a sample equation, quite a short one, and, while it took most of the morning, I managed to solve it, as she herself confirmed in a later, algorithmically-derived exchange. Our rapport, I should say, has become so good via this method, that it is no longer necessary for me to write down our conversations. I can carry them on internally and transcribe them later. When I have a sufficiently good grasp of base seight calculus, I can contact Jordan and deduct her from water machine.

It's a simple as that.

Vector simulator – water machine is impersonal programmed in base seight, you are trying to countermand it using personal program in base seight, it won't work.

Correction: it will work, because base seight carries the impersonal function just as the music carries base ten, freeing up the program to re-establish personal lineation and segmentarity: name, gender, age, nationality, and so on, thus generating the person again.

Vector simulator – personal identity contingent on physical transfer vessel, stop.

Correction: I won't stop, I'll get pregnant and give birth to her. I'll find her cousin's baby.

Transanimation to transfer vessel, no division.

I'll make her a person.

Everyone has to be a person.

No one escapes.

There is no water machine. There is no water machine. There is no water machine.

About the Author

Michael Cisco published ten novels including *The Divinity Student, The Great Lover, The Narrator, ANIMAL MONEY,* and *UNLANGUAGE,* and a short story collection called *Secret Hours.* His short fiction has appeared in: *The Thackery T. Lambshead Pocket Guide to Eccentric and Discredited Diseases, Lovecraft Unbound, Black Wings, Blood and Other Cravings, THE WEIRD, The Grimscribe's Puppets,* and *Aickman's Heirs,* among others. He teaches at CUNY Hostos.

GRIMSCRIBE PRESS

Milton Keynes UK
Ingram Content Group UK Ltd.
UKHW041449250923
429348UK00003B/155